MW00940288

Keeper. She grew up in Argentina, but life eventually led her to live in London, the city that was her home for many years.

She has an MA in Creative Writing from Kingston University. She has been an editor and writer for several news organizations and magazines, both in London and Argentina; and she has taught creative writing at Universidad de San Andrés.

Like many of the characters in this book, she has a healthy craving for wild journeys and unforgettable adventures. She also has an unfading love for words, language and the magic of storytelling.

Visit www.veronicadelvallebooks.com for more information.

THE BOOK OF FOUR JOURNEYS

Veronica del Valle

SilverWood

Published in 2021 by SilverWood Books

SilverWood Books Ltd
14 Small Street, Bristol, BS1 1DE, United Kingdom
www.silverwoodbooks.co.uk

ISBN 978-1-80042-044-1 (paperback)
ISBN 978-1-80042-045-8 (ebook)

British Library Cataloguing in Publication Data
A CIP catalogue record for this book is
available from the British Library

Page design and typesetting by SilverWood Books

For my brother

Contents

Alfalfa Spooly

I have a story to tell you. A story about a well-kept secret. I'm not particularly fond of secrets but I found myself entangled in this mysterious turn of events by accident and without forewarning.

Any sensible storyteller would agree with what the famous King of Hearts once said: "Begin at the beginning, and go on till you come to the end: then stop." I have always followed this advice when telling a story, so that is what I will do for you now.

I hope you will stay with me until the end. But at this stage in our journey, I am not sure what said end will be like once we get there.

The Beginning

I suppose the first thing I should do is introduce myself. My name is Alfalfa Spooly. Many call me Alfie, usually the very old or the very young. Some call me Alfalfa-Spooly, all together, as if it were one long single word instead of a first name and a surname. Personally, I like plain Alfalfa. I feel that's who I am.

Aside from being Alfalfa, I am also a postman. Well, that is actually my job, not who I am, but at the end of the day, what we do every day defines us probably more than we would like. So, I like to say I *am* a postman as opposed to saying I work as a postman.

So... I'm Alfalfa and I'm a postman. A very good one if I may add. For those of you who aren't familiar with this trade, it basically means I deliver letters. One might think it sounds like an easy task to tackle, but once I've detailed the Five Famous Traits needed to be a good postman, you might think differently. To be a good postman, one has to follow the five rules below:

1) Have a good memory. If you know by heart the names of the streets and people, you save a great deal of time. This leads to our next quality.

2) Be organised. If you are not, you lose mail and you deliver letters to the wrong homes, which can lead to all sorts of trouble.

3) Have a sunny disposition, even to those who get mad when you deliver telephone bills, break-up letters and other unwanted mail.

4) Be fit. A true postman either walks or cycles.

5) Last but not least, be good at the art of deciphering. Most people's handwriting looks like doodles instead of real words.

But now, enough about me. Let's dive into the story.

On the day it all began, I woke up thinking about trait number two. I wanted to work up a system to simplify my not so simple job of dealing with so many items and so many places. After only a few attempts, I gave up as it was too early in the morning. The roosters hadn't even started crowing.

I had a bowl of porridge for breakfast, grabbed my messenger bag and postman's cap and walked to the post office. I am used to working in all weathers, but luckily for me it wasn't a rainy morning; it was a bright and sunny one.

All was quiet in Yellow, the town where I live and work. Yellow. Yes, just like the colour. It is long and narrow, almost the shape of a sponge finger biscuit. The town has four very long avenues and twenty-two very short streets, which cross the aforementioned very long four avenues. Yellow nestles in a valley surrounded by spiky hills.

I know every single street in my town; I could draw a map of it with my eyes closed. This, of course, is made easier because every street in Yellow is named after something that is...you probably guessed it: yellow. As a result, we have Mustard Avenue, Saffron Road, Cheese Alley, Daffodil Boulevard, Lemon Street, Egg Yolk Lane, Builder's Helmet Mews, Rubber Duck Roundabout and Banana Cobbled Street among others. I live on Butter Street, and I walk down Corn Road to get to work.

I was the first one to arrive at the post office. Well, as a matter of fact, I am always the first to arrive. Although there are only three of us (Nora the receptionist, Lucas the stamp seller, and me), I always beat them, but not on purpose. I just like waking up early.

I opened the windows, sat at my desk and sorted through the mail. I like to map my route before each day's delivery. I also like to look at the handwriting and guess what the letters are about: is it a love letter? Is it a postcard from a trip? Does the letter carry bad news? Or good news? I always find myself hoping it's the latter.

Initially, at first sight, nothing looked out of the ordinary. But then a strange envelope landed in my hands. It was addressed to our town's milliner, Kinsley. Now, this wouldn't necessarily be unusual. You see, Kinsley is so talented at his craft, he doesn't just make hats for the folks in Yellow. People from all over the globe write to him with all manner of hat requests. But without fail, every single one of these letters is always addressed in the same manner:

Kinsley, the world's most famous milliner

22 Canary Road

Yellow

However, the letter I was holding in my hands read:

Kinsley, the YELLOW hatmaker

22 Canary Road

Yellow

If that wasn't strange enough, the letter also had two other messages written in capital letters across each top corner.

One said: HUSH HUSH

The other: HIGHLY IMPORTANT

To make matters stranger still, the envelope had no sender. No information whatsoever of who had written to Kinsley.

I decided not to jump to hasty conclusions, but to start my working day. I planned my route in a way that would allow me to deliver Kinsley's letter last. All the mail was chucked in my messenger bag and my postman's cap was on. As I was getting ready to leave, Nora and Lucas arrived. Nora was finishing a croissant and Lucas was panting, having run all the way from his house to get to the post office ahead of me.

"Oh, man," Lucas whined when he clapped eyes on me.

"I don't know why you get so upset about it," Nora said between bites. "Just accept the fact that we will never get here before Alfalfa, be happy and arrive late."

"I'm gonna do it one day, Alfalfa. One day I'll get here before you," he said, shaking a fist and snarling unconvincingly.

We all laughed, but I decided not to tell them anything about Kinsley's odd letter. I didn't want to start a fuss over nothing. Maybe Kinsley's client was in a hurry to get his hat and had become confused about how to address the envelope. And maybe he had put his contact information on the letter. As Nora and Lucas settled down to start the day, I scurried out of the post office.

My first stop was at Nicolette Monroe's house on Sunflower Street. Her fiancé, who lived far away, sent her love letters every week. And even when he came to visit her, he still wrote her letters and I still delivered them. Then I walked to Gold Lane to deliver what looked like a very formal document to Mr Mooligan, the headmaster at Sunshine Middle School, and then to Miss Roselyn's house on Sand Lane.

At noon, I stopped by the Middle Traffic Light Café and had a sandwich followed by a slice of vanilla flan for lunch. Then I went straight to Bee Boulevard where I delivered a kitchenware catalogue to the Ragoon family and lastly, I dropped off a package at Mr Lalonde on Sun Street. Canary Road was right next to Sun Street, so it was only a two-minute walk to Kinsley's shop.

*

A bell at the door to the hat shop would tinkle to let Kinsley know there was a new customer. He was behind the counter, deeply engaged in his work. A mop of grey hair covered his wrinkled forehead and hid his tawny-brown eyes. He was stitching a large feather to a very elegant musketeer hat, but as soon as he heard the bell tinkle, he looked up.

"Alfalfa Spooly, good afternoon!"

"Good afternoon."

"What do you have for me today?"

"Well," I started, stumped by what to say next, so I just reached inside my messenger bag and handed him the letter.

Kinsley looked at it. He seemed surprised, yet not puzzled at all. After a few moments of simply staring at it, he whispered, "I haven't received a letter like this in such a long time." There was a trace of a nostalgic smile, which lingered in his eyes and flittered across his face.

"What do you mean *like this*?" I asked him.

Kinsley didn't say anything at first. He bit

his lip as he looked at me and seemed about to say something, but then not, but then he did. "Can you keep a secret, Alfalfa Spooly, and never tell it to anyone?" Kinsley dropped his voice to a hoarse whisper and checked the shelves heaped with velvet-dressed hat boxes and all manner of headwear, as if each might creep closer to the edge of its shelf to overhear our conversation.

"I think I can." I looked about too, eyeing a fancy vermillion fascinator beadily.

"I think you can too. Come with me. I want to show you something."

Behind the counter there was a small door. Kinsley produced a large well-oiled key, attached by ribbon to the pocket of his sateen paisley waistcoat. He then opened the door and we stooped to walk through it. Behind the small door there was a huge room. Hats of all sorts were piled haphazardly everywhere you looked: top hats, cowboy hats, porkpie hats, trilby hats, fez hats, newsboy caps and a few berets.

"This is where I work," Kinsley said to me. There was a big square desk in the middle of the room, hat stands surrounding it like a guard of honour. On top of the desk were scissors, pins, thimbles, tailor's chalk, some sort of special steamer, and more needles than Kinsley could use in a lifetime, long and short, thick and thin. Kinsley later said they were called millinery needles, made especially for sewing straw and felt. There were two sewing machines, but Kinsley confided that the real masterpieces were always hand-stitched.

We walked to the end of the room. An old wardrobe leant against one of the corners. Kinsley looked at me again.

"Are you sure you can keep a secret, Alfalfa Spooly? Never tell it to anyone?"

"I think I can."

"I think you can too. But I need to be sure."

Kinsley glanced at the wardrobe, so I did the same. As he opened it, a woody scent seeped into the room.

Inside, there were seven shelves. On top of each shelf there were seven yellow bowler hats, with small brims and a matching yellow band around the crown. The rounded, hard-topped hats were made of what appeared to be a bright yellow wool-felt. I was certain this was no ordinary wool-felt hat, because ordinary wool-felt hats don't glow with their own golden light.

"These are special hats," Kinsley said.

"Are they terribly expensive?"

"No, not really."

"I see." But I wasn't really seeing, so I rephrased my question. "They're beaming light. How do they do that?"

The shop's bell tinkled. Kinsley looked at the small door. I looked at him.

"I'll be right back." He dashed off to see who had arrived.

I was both very puzzled and very intrigued. Equally, one might say. My glance took me from the little door to the big square desk with the scissors and needles, then straight back to the wardrobe and the yellow hats.

I came closer. My nose was less than an inch from one of them. I touched it with my index finger. Nothing happened. So, I lightly stroked the brim. I had never touched such abundant shininess before. It felt warm, soothing, fleecy-soft. I grabbed it with both hands and was about to put it on when Kinsley walked back in. I returned the hat before he saw me and stood straight and irreproachable as a soldier.

"Sorry about that," Kinsley said as he walked back to me. "It was Miss Monroe. She wanted a red velvet cloche hat as her suitor is coming next week."

Then, with the highest respect I had ever witnessed, Kinsley looked at the first yellow hat on the first shelf. Carefully and unhurriedly, he took hold of it and closed the wardrobe. He hesitated for a minute before asking what he finally asked. "Would you deliver this hat for me?"

"Is that for the person who wrote the letter?" I asked.

Kinsley nodded.

"Um…" I liked the idea of making a secret delivery. It already felt like a mission. So, after a few more carefully planned Ums, I answered full-on, "Yes! Where would I need to deliver it?"

"Beyond the spiky hills of Yellow, there's a forsaken road. At the end of the forsaken road, there is a river. Across the river, there is a town called Blue. In the bluest house of Blue lives a man named Phineas. This yellow hat is for him."

The next day was Saturday. I figured I had the whole weekend to carry out my mission.

"I can do it. I can deliver the yellow hat to Phineas in the bluest house of Blue."

The Middle

I stood at the foot of the spiky hills. I had my postman's cap on and my messenger bag was on my shoulder, with the yellow hat in it. I looked up at the sharpened brown peaks. They seemed so far away, and this was only the beginning of my journey. What was behind the spiky hills? How forsaken was the forsaken road? How wide was the river I had to cross to get to Blue?

"How am I going to do this?" I said aloud. The question slipped out of me, almost involuntarily.

"One step after the other," a soft voice answered.

It came from above. I glanced warily that way. When my eyes found the voice, I saw it belonged to a boy with grey eyes and, what seemed to me, a spontaneous smile.

"That's the way my goats do it," the boy said as he descended from a ragged boulder. He was surrounded by seven goats and he walked carefully, probing the ground with a large crooked stick he'd clearly fashioned himself. "They take their time because they are in no rush. Rock by rock, my goats climb all the way to the top, and believe me, to the very top they get."

"One step after the other," I repeated. It

sounded reasonable. "Thank you. I'm Alfalfa, by the way. And I'm a postman."

"I'm Ollie, and I'm a goat herder."

"Are these your goats?"

"Uh-huh. These are Peggy, Pierce, Parker, Peyton, Pim, Poppy and Pablo," Ollie said, pointing to each one accordingly.

We began to climb the spiky hill together, Ollie, the seven goats and I. The goats walked in front of us, one step after the other, and we followed.

"So, your job as a goat herder is to take care of Peggy, Pierce, Parker, Peyton, Pim, Poppy and Pablo?"

"Good memory," Ollie said. "Yes, I have to tend and rear them, but truth be told, they also take care of me."

"They do?" I asked, as if it was not possible.

"Of course!" he said, as if it were the most obvious thing in the world.

"You live alone here in the hills?"

"If you count my goats as company, which I do, then no, I don't live alone. But if you are talking about other human beings, then yes, I'm mostly alone. But I like it that way. I have plenty of time to ponder over things that matter. And to do that, you must be alone. It's easier to think."

"Huh…"

"May I ask you something?" Ollie said, and when I nodded, he went on. "What was troubling you when we met?"

"I have agreed to do something that I'm not so sure I can do."

"What is so impossible to do?"

I had given my word to keep Kinsley's secret come what may, so I decided to tell Ollie what little I could. "I have to go beyond Yellow and into Blue to deliver a package."

"Aren't you a postman?"

"But I have never been outside my hometown."

"Are you a good postman?"

"I think I am, yes. I am a master in the Five Famous Traits any great postman should have."

"Then you will do a fine job no matter the place. You're not just a good postman in Yellow. Look at Pablo," Ollie said, pointing up. I followed his finger until my eyes met the goat high up the hill. "Look at the way he approaches that precipice. He moves with such ease. You should do the same."

"But Pablo is a goat and I am a person."

"I have never left these spiky hills," Ollie said, "but if I ever did, I would try to do as Pablo does and venture into the unknown with ease."

When Ollie finished, I realised we were standing alongside Pablo on the precipice at the top of the spiky hills. I could see Yellow to the east and the forsaken road to the west. It was spine-chilling to be standing at the very peak. I had never seen the sky so close. It looked as if I could stretch out my hand, shred a piece of cloud, cram it in my mouth and eat it like cotton candy.

But instead of this, we sat down. Ollie split a loaf of bread and offered me half. I took a huge bite. Ollie took a small one. Three of the goats had settled near us, their hooves tucked neatly under their bodies. The other four had made their way to a solitary shrub and were munching at its leaves.

"This place is out of this world," I said, looking into the distance.

"The greatest thing is that it isn't. All this," Ollie said, pointing across to the spiky hills, down towards the valley surrounding Yellow and up to the sky beyond his fingertips, "is *our* world. Even the simplest things can be special things."

I thought of the yellow hats and what Kinsley had told me when I had asked why the hats were special.

"They have powers," Kinsley had said as he wrapped up the hat for Phineas.

"Powers? What kind of powers?"

"That is for the hat's owner to decide. When

you get a yellow hat, you can infuse it with one power of your choosing."

"Are you telling me that the person who has one of these hats can get any power they wish for?"

"While they are wearing the hat, yes."

"So, a person could fly while wearing one?"

"If they so wished, yes they could. But, funnily enough, no one has ever asked for that power."

Kinsley led me to a buttoned leather sofa that was old and battered in a corner of his workshop and we sat down.

"What have they asked for?"

"Many different powers were chosen for many different reasons: a diplomat once asked for the power to speak in eleven different languages. A coconut lover wanted a hat to enable her to climb palm trees like a monkey. And a sceptical detective chose the power to know when people were lying to him no matter the size of the lie."

"So, I could be the best kung fu fighter and the greatest chess player if I was sporting one of these yellow hats?"

"You would have to choose. A yellow hat can only have one power."

"How can a person make such a choice?"

"It isn't easy, and not only because you have to pick only one, but because you must be careful with what you wish for."

"Why?"

"Once there was a librarian who loved to read. When she got her yellow hat, she asked to have a perfect memory so she could remember all the stories she liked. But having a perfect memory meant she could remember everything. Every word she had ever read, or spoken, or heard. She became overwhelmed by the sheer amount of memories that were now stored in her mind. Her head became so heavy she was unable to stand upright anymore. Eventually, she had no choice but to stop wearing the hat. That goes to show how precise you have to be when you pick your power."

"Oh..." I pictured the librarian with her heavy head. It wasn't a pretty picture. Thankfully, another question popped into my head. "How come I've never seen anyone wear a yellow hat on the streets?"

"When the owner puts the yellow hat on, it appears to become an ordinary black bowler hat. Just like any other hat."

"And what if it lands on the head of someone who wishes to do wrong?"

"I like your questions, Alfalfa Spooly. To answer your last one: the hat wouldn't work. Yellow hats hate any kind of evil. They even dislike petty mischief. They bounce off the heads of naughty people."

The four goats had stripped the lonely shrub bare, leaving only a few half-nibbled leaves. All that was left of the loaf of bread were a few crumbs on my trousers, which I shook off as we stood up.

"Well, now you just have to walk down,"

Ollie said, "which is always easier than climbing up."

I said goodbye to him and the seven goats.

Before I knew it, Yellow and the spiky hills were far behind me and I was walking the forsaken road. Even though I hadn't opened my messenger bag since I'd left, I unhooked the straps and unzipped it to check the yellow hat was still there. It was. Good. I closed my bag and journeyed on.

The forsaken road was so deserted it gave me plenty of time to ruminate about plenty of matters. All of which revolved around the yellow hats. The first matter that popped into my mind was: how does one set about creating a hat with the ability to host a power?

Before leaving Kinsley's shop, I had asked him: "How do you make them?"

And he had answered: "Well, that is a whole other secret. It is one I cannot share, like a secret within a secret. When I mastered the art of hat-making, my teacher passed on the ancient knowledge of yellow hat crafting. A combination of difficult manoeuvres, rare cloths and intricate stitches. It is a combination I cannot reveal."

It goes without saying that this only made me more curious, but I guess there are some things in life we'll never know...unless you have a yellow hat and ask to know all the secret things. That brought me to a second matter: ever since Kinsley had told me about these hats, I had wondered, what would my power be?

What about the power to foresee the future? I could avoid all ugly events. But then again, there's something nice about not knowing what will happen tomorrow. Other options that I considered were the power to eat all the candy and ice cream I want without ever getting a stomach ache, and the power to be awesome at every sport.

Now, these powers had to do with things I liked, but what about powers that would help me dodge things I disliked? Like a power to *never ever* have to visit the dentist again. Or the power to solve *any* and *all* maths problems. Although that would have come in handy when I was at school, but not so much now. What would I need now? If I had the power to run *really* fast, I could deliver the letters in five minutes each day. But I discarded that idea. I liked my job and wouldn't want to do it in five minutes and be done with it.

As I pondered, I looked around and saw how dry everything around me was. The ground looked as if it had been weathered by years of storm winds. There were dunes of searing sand steaming on both sides of the road. The sun was definitely not friendly on the forsaken road. It was exceptionally hot and extraordinarily bright, with only a few scorched shrubs struggling to survive in this wasteland. I shaded my eyes and kept walking.

It was only when I thought the sun was my worst enemy and things couldn't get worse that I spotted something in the distance.

"Is that what I think it is?" I said out loud, truly hoping it wasn't. But then I stopped walking and looked closer. Yep. That was a raging tornado swirling towards me. If I'd had a power at that moment, I would have chosen to control the weather and make that wild funnel-shaped monster disappear. But I couldn't so instead I ran.

I ran and I ran and I ran. But the tornado kept getting closer, moving faster than I could. My heart pounded in turbo mode. Without my bike, postman trait number four – *Be fit* – was failing to suffice under these circumstances.

I turned my head to see how close the tornado was, tripped and fell face-first on the gravelly forsaken road. My hands cushioned the blow, my postman's cap flew off and my messenger bag tangled around my arm. Jumping to my feet, I jerked my arm free and slung my bag across my shoulder. My entire body ached, a pain that vanished into thin air when I saw the tornado right behind me. But I had to get my postman's cap back; it was my badge of honour. No one is a real postman without it. I darted to where it was skipping, at the base of the tornado's wild winds.

The tornado chased me, and I chased the cap which danced away from me. As soon as I got closer to it, a gust of wind plucked it farther away. The cap flew wildly in front of me, moving up and down, left and right. I knew I would have to act as stealthily and swiftly as a ninja. When the hat flew right in front of me, I aimed, shot my arm towards it, and snatched it back. "YES!" My yell of victory was probably heard across the spiky hills by Nora and Lucas. I put on my postman's cap and kept running.

Out of the corner of my eye, I saw something much faster than me. A flock of ostriches. They sprinted past me, away from the tornado's path.

"Jump on me," one of them boomed, "or the tornado will swallow you up!"

I had always been a long-time opponent of doing things without careful planning, but that day on the forsaken road I had to chuck logic away and act without thinking about the consequences. I closed my eyes and leapt.

But, even with my eyes firmly shut, I landed on the ostrich and held tight to his long neck with one hand and my messenger bag with the other. The flock dashed away from the tornado. I'd never been on a space rocket before but I was pretty sure we were moving at the speed of light.

An interesting fact I didn't know, yet now I do (and probably won't forget), is that tornados do not follow a specific route. They are awfully fickle. Luckily for the ostriches and me, this one decided to change direction. When we approached the river, it veered off to the north and had soon disappeared into the distance.

At the bank of the river, I slipped gingerly off the ostrich. My legs wobbled, my head span, and my ears rang. I could barely hear what one of the ostriches was telling me. From the few words I caught, I fathomed that the freckled girl in the white canoe could take me across the river.

I reckoned I had heard wrong, or maybe the ostrich was a bit cuckoo? But as it turned out, I had

heard right, and the ostrich was sane. As I wobbled towards the grassy sloping bank, I stumbled upon a doe-eyed girl with a face chock-full of freckles and glossy curly hair that defied the rules of gravity. She was sitting by the shore eating an apple and feeding breadcrumbs to three nesting ducks. Beside her, there was a white birchbark canoe.

She turned around. "Would you like an apple?" she said.

It was only then I realised how hungry I was. She handed me a pinkish-red apple. I thanked her, and while I devoured the crunchy, juicy, honey-sweet fruit, she told me she had named the ducks Smith, Baldwin and Pippin because apples were her favourite food and that the river was called Viridian, on account of its colour. The last thing she told me was her own name, Bluebell.

"Mine is Alfalfa," I said, slurring my words, still shaken from the ostrich ride.

But she must have understood because she asked, "Where are you heading, Alfalfa?"

"To Blue." I knelt by the shore, cupped my hands and took a draught of fresh water. "I've heard you could take me across the river in your canoe?"

"Do you have the silver token to get across the Viridian?"

"No, I don't. Where do I buy it?"

"You don't buy a silver token. You win one, over there." Bluebell pointed to a giant hoop about a hundred yards from where we were sitting. "Speak to Mr Littlefair."

As I walked over, I saw that the giant hoop was in fact a big carnival wheel. An old, lanky man with a wonky nose sat on a stool beside it. He was drinking condensed milk out of a can and didn't give me the chance to ask if he was Mr Littlefair.

"Want a silver token?" he mumbled, swigging from the can of condensed milk.

"Yes, please."

"Spin the wheel."

"Excuse me?"

"You spin the wheel. You get a challenge. If you pass the challenge, you win a silver token." He wiped his mouth with the back of his hand.

I looked at the big carnival wheel; it was divided into seventy-four different pie wedges. Each wedge had a challenge.

"I guess I have no other choice," I said.

"I guess not," the old, lanky man said snappily. He looked as if he was about to run out of patience with the world and consequently with me, so I grabbed one of the metal dowels and spun the carnival wheel down hard. I watched as the wheel turned around and around and around, and heard the *plick-plick-plick-plick* of the metal dowels against the iron rod that would mark my fate.

As it slowed down, I was able to read the challenges as they spun past my eyes.

Plick.

Challenge: What is 5,349 to the third power equal to?

Plick.

Challenge: Recite three sonnets, a villanelle and a sestina.

Plick.

Challenge: Dance a fandango, a polka and a tango.

Plick.

"I'm never getting across the Viridian," I said quietly to myself. Blood was hissing in my ears as I waited and hot tears streamed down my face.

Plick... Plick... Plick... The wheel had almost stopped when I saw the next wedge.

Challenge: Name ten yellow things in less than ten seconds.

"YES!" I shouted. A glimmer of hope sparked inside me. "STOP! STOP THERE, PLEASE!"

Plick.

"NOOO!" My heart sank. I grabbed my head in my hands and shut my eyes so tight I thought I might not be able to open them again. Then I heard the old man speak.

"Lucky boy..."

"What? What do you mean *Lucky boy*?" I said, as I opened my eyes and looked at the wheel.

"You got the Wacky Woodchuck Wedge."

"What is the Wacky Woodchuck Wedge?"

"It's the wildcard of the wheel. Here." He tossed me a silver token. I caught it mid-air and sprinted back to the river.

Bluebell was still feeding breadcrumbs to Smith, Baldwin and Pippin. She heard me running and turned around.

"All right! You got a token! Excellent! What challenge did you get?" Bluebell asked.

"I got the Wacky Woodchuck Wedge."

"Lucky you! I'm glad you won. Canoe rides are meant to be shared." She winked at me. "We must hurry though. It's almost nightfall, and when the moon comes out, the river likes to get a little wild and it's not so easy to row on choppy waters."

We pushed the white canoe into the river and jumped in.

If you've never been inside one, you probably won't know this, but balancing inside a canoe is difficult and dangerous. Every small movement seems to tilt the boat to the point of capsizing. I sat down as fast as I could to avoid a catastrophe. Bluebell sat at the stern and I was near the bow.

"If you show me how, I can grab an oar and paddle with you," I said.

"Okay. Grip the paddle with both hands. Reach forward and plant the paddle's blade in the water. Now, pull it back towards you. Repeat."

I followed Bluebell's instructions to the letter. Every few strokes, we switched sides.

The water of the Viridian was cool, graceful and, as its name suggested, dark green, but a bright kind of dark, like a spring green. The current tried to push us off our course, but we pushed back. We dodged around patches of tall reeds here and there. The river was wide; it took us a while to cross it. I saw trout, bream and a catfish with long whiskers. I had never seen any of these fish before, but Bluebell taught me their names and all about them.

Just as a full moon was crawling up the sky, we arrived on the far side of the river. At a short dock we tied the canoe. I spotted a town in the near distance.

"That's Blue," she said.

"Thank you for helping me get here."

"Thank you for paddling with me."

There were other things I could have said and asked. I only knew her name. But to tell the truth, that's all I needed to know; it was the way I wanted to remember her: the freckled girl who took me across the river in her white canoe.

A narrow, winding country road led me to Blue. The town was quaint, postcard-perfect and monochrome. Some of the houses were small, others were big. Some had dormer windows, others had chimneys. Some looked like bungalows, others resembled castles. But no matter what its shape or size, every house in Blue was painted in a particular shade of said colour: cerulean, indigo, ultramarine, periwinkle, turquoise, and others for which I didn't have a name.

All I had to do now was find the bluest one. But what did *bluest* actually mean? The brightest blue? The darkest blue? Which one of all the colours was the truest blue?

The full moon lit up the town. I walked in silence through the empty cobbled streets. It felt like being a detective, searching for clues that would tell me which of all these dwellings was Phineas's home. I scanned every house, but I found nothing, not a single piece of evidence. My investigation seemed to be leading nowhere.

I was about to take a break when I came across a little cottage painted royal blue. Surely, that had to be the quintessential blue.

Had I found it?

I stood straight, rearranged my postman's cap and knocked on the door of the bluest house in Blue.

Almost, Nearly, the End

So here we are, almost at the end. I hope you are still with me. Because, as I told you at the beginning, I don't know how this story is going to end and I could use some company while I find out.

As I stand waiting, I check my messenger bag once more to make sure the yellow hat is there. It is. Good.

The door in the bluest house of Blue squeaks as it opens. I see a man with a wizened face, his thatch of white hair springing up like a dandelion. He looks at me and smiles. I think he knows why I'm at his door.

"Are you Phineas?" I ask.

"I am," he answers. "Do you have a package for me?"

"I do. My name is Alfalfa Spooly and I have a special delivery from Kinsley, the yellow hatmaker."

Our eyes meet with a knowing look.

"Come on in then, Alfalfa." He waves me

inside his little royal-blue cottage. With the help of a cane made out of bamboo, he walks at the pace of a tortoise.

We go into the kitchen. It's small but warm and a sweet, buttery scent fills the whole room.

"I made them this afternoon." Phineas brings out a tray with shell-shaped madeleines. We sit down at the kitchen table. "Help yourself." He pushes the tray towards me with the slowest of movements. I grab one and take a bite. They are in fact lighter than clouds, the most delicious thing I've ever eaten. Two bites and the madeleine is gone. That's how good they are. While I eat three more, I tell him all about my journey: about the spiky hills, Ollie and the seven goats; the forsaken road, the tornado and the ostriches; the Viridian river, Bluebell and her white canoe. He listens.

Now it is time to complete my mission. I open my bag and take out the package wrapped by Kinsley. Phineas's eyelids flicker with delight. He unwraps it as fast as he can and grabs the hat with both hands, the way a little boy holds his first toy.

"My yellow hat!"

"Do you know which power you'll choose?"

"I do." There is a twinkle in his eyes, full of impish glee, and a faint curve to his lips reveals a cheeky smile.

But before telling me his choice, he tells me his story. "I was born here in Blue, in this very cottage. I've lived here all my life. I have never travelled anywhere. I have never had any stories of my own, not one adventure I can claim to my name. And now I'm too old to go out into the world." He pauses. Following the zigzagging carvings of the wooden kitchen table with his index finger, he sighs. "I have read countless books and I've found great adventures there, but now my sight is failing and I can't read anymore. That's where my yellow hat comes in: I want to have endless imagination. That way I'll be able to travel, be part of great stories, and become a dauntless adventurer…if only inside my mind."

"Why don't you ask for the power to be younger again?"

"I could, but I won't."

"Because it wouldn't be fair?"

"The choices I made have made me who I am. One life was given to me and I have lived it here in Blue. I can't re-do it. I can, however, make the most of the time I have left. Besides, I have a sneaky feeling my imagination will take me to places that don't exist anywhere in this world."

"I wish you wonderful journeys, Phineas."

"Alfalfa?" Phineas says as I grab my messenger bag and put on my postman's cap.

"Yes?"

"Would you like a yellow hat?"

"Excuse me?" I drop the messenger bag and sit back down.

"Only the owner of a yellow hat can tell you how to get a yellow hat. Remember the letter I sent to Kinsley?"

"Aha."

"In that letter I had to write the secret words to enable me to be the owner of a yellow hat."

"So, you need the sealed stamp of approval from a previous owner?"

"Exactly. And each owner gets to pick only one person."

"You are choosing me?"

"Yes. You have brought me joy today. More than you can imagine. Your delivery has made this day a very good day. But there's more. The owner must choose a person with three qualities: wisdom, chivalry and the right amount of pizzazz. You have proved you have all three qualities. I choose you."

"I'm honoured." Phineas is about to tell me the secret words to get a yellow hat when I say, "No."

"You're not ready?"

"It isn't that I'm not ready. It's just that I don't think I want a yellow hat."

"What do you mean?" Phineas's head tilts to the side and his brows draw close together.

"I already have one power. The power not to need anything from a yellow hat."

"But a yellow hat can give you *any* power you want."

"If I had asked for the power to jump over mountains, I wouldn't have had to climb the spiky hills. And I wouldn't have met Ollie and the seven goats. If I had had the power to control the weather, I wouldn't have felt what it's like to run like the wind on the back of an ostrich. If I'd had a yellow hat to be super mighty, I wouldn't have learned how to paddle a canoe with Bluebell, the girl with the freckled face. There's nothing I can ask that will make me happier than I am today. Thank you so much, Phineas, but I have to respectfully decline."

Phineas smiled.

"Why are you smiling?" I ask.

And this is what he answers: "Because those are the secret words. You can have a yellow hat when you know you don't need one. You can now, if you wish, choose to ask Kinsley for a yellow hat. You hold the answer in your hands. You decide."

Mumik & Pimnik

Day One

In the Northernmost Part of the World

Mumik Opipok opened his eyes and knew straight away what he had to do. It would take courage, loads of it. He would have to summon it all because he was not the most confident person. In fact, Mumik Opipok's life had so far been dotted with doubtful moments: should I fish with my fishing rod or with my net? Should I walk to the lake or go on my sledge? Should I wear my white scarf or my chequered one? Should I make fish fillet or seafood chowder for lunch? For each choice, Mumik debated with himself for hours, and when he finally made a choice, he would second-guess it one more time. Just in case.

But not that morning. Mumik was more confident than he had ever been about any decision. In fact, he had made up his mind as soon as he'd heard what the White Bright Sprite had told him. He knew what he had to do. There was no other way to look at it.

From that moment, his day was dedicated to getting everything ready for his journey. He borrowed an old sailboat courtesy of a former sailor-turned-igloo-maker who had a spare boat. It was rusty, but it floated and that was what mattered. The former sailor-turned-igloo-maker taught Mumik the essentials of sailing: the menaces one can find at sea, how to read charts, how to trim the mainsail and how to use a sextant to let the stars guide him to his destination.

When the sailing class was over, Mumik walked home. He lived in an igloo of bluish blocks of ice in the Northernmost Part of the World. "The top of the globe," he liked to say. This was a place shrouded in eternal winter, which meant it was always very *very* cold, but also very *very* snowy, silvery white and spotless. His good friend, Koko, a wordy and cunning Arctic fox, was waiting by his front door.

"All ready?" Koko asked.

"Almost," Mumik answered. "Where are Sesi and Sila?"

"Around the back of the igloo, sleeping like true grey wolves," Koko said.

Mumik went inside and packed some items of clothing, his fishing rod, some cans of food and many bottles of water. He was aware he was not the best planner, but he figured he would be fine with the things he had selected. Before sunset, everything was ready. He would leave in the morning.

When the full moon lit the sky, Mumik went outside and woke up Sesi and Sila.

"Come on, my friends, time for one last ride."

Mumik put on a beanie hat and tightened the knot of his chequered scarf. He gave the reins of his sledge a quick yank and off they went. Sesi and Sila blazed across the snowy slopes. Mumik deftly steered the sledge to the left and to the right; the runners drew a zigzagging sketch, which was soon covered by fresh snowfall.

As they neared the village, Mumik chose his first song. His voice rose and fell, and was carried through the wintry air, spreading across the white land. As the Lullaby Chanter of the Northernmost Part of the World, Mumik Opipok sang three lullabies every night to help all the children across the north fall asleep swiftly and dream only good dreams. It was a task he had been appointed by the Elders on the day he was born.

As he began his third lullaby of the night, a soothing song that spoke of farewells, Mumik could not help but think of the White Bright Sprite. Only a day had passed since his birthday, but since then everything had changed.

On each birthday, every being in the Northernmost Part of the World received a wish from the White Bright Sprite. She lived in the Ivory Ash, a tree with stalactites instead of branches and snowflakes instead of leaves. Following this tradition, Mumik went to see her as he did every year.

"Good morning, Mumik Opipok, and happy birthday to you today," the White Bright Sprite said with the softest of voices.

"Good morning, White Bright Sprite, thank you for your kind words. I've had a happy day so far." Mumik was always a little nervous when speaking to her.

"Today is your twelfth winter birthday, is that right?" the White Bright Sprite asked.

"Yes."

"What wish would you like for this new year of your life?"

Mumik had been thinking long and hard about this over the past few days. "I would like to know something I do not yet know."

The White Bright Sprite looked at him in awe. No one had ever asked for something of this sort. Everyone always wanted *something*, as in a *thing* of *some kind*: a new sledge, a pet puffin, a very warm coat. But nobody had ever asked for knowledge they did not yet possess.

"I like your wish." The White Bright Sprite paused and thought for a moment. She seemed to hesitate before finally saying, "I have something, but it may be a harsh truth to hear. Would you still want it?"

Should I say yes or no? Mumik wondered, doubting as he always did. He jumped from *yes* to *no* and from *no* to *yes* at least fourteen times, before he finally chose. "Yes."

"Very well then."

Mumik held his breath and clenched his hands. His nails made small crescents in the palms of his hands.

"The day you were born," the White Bright Sprite began, "you were not born alone. You were born hand in hand with a sibling."

Mumik stared at the White Bright Sprite. He opened his mouth but nothing came out. He felt as if he stayed open-mouthed for an ice age.

"What are you telling me?" These were the only words he was able to utter.

"I'm telling you that you have a twin," the White Bright Sprite said. "Her name is Pimnik."

"Pimnik…" Mumik whispered, looking

down at the snow. His heart quickened to double speed. He glanced up at the White Bright Sprite. "But how have I never met her?!"

"Because you remained here and Pimnik was sent to be the Lullaby Chanter of the Southernmost Part of the World."

"Why?"

"You both have voices that can cut through any ugly thought and brighten any gloomy day. It is a rare and exceptional gift."

"No! I meant why were we torn apart?"

"I told you. You were born to be Lullaby Chanters."

"But we were also born to be a brother and a sister! A family!" Tears welled up in Mumik's eyes. He was sad and angry and he did not want to feel any of those emotions on his birthday. He was painfully torn: a part of him wished he had never voiced his wish, while another part of him wished more than anything to know *everything* about Pimnik.

66

"You're right, Mumik Opipok, it was unfair, but it is what the Elders decided. They are sages, as you well know. Their wisdom is unparalleled, as is their goodwill to do what's best for our community. When they make a decision, we always respect it. Decisions are not always easy. Sometimes they must choose between two equally important things."

"It's still unfair!" Mumik cried. He felt his salty tears freeze as they ran down his cheeks. A wretched knot gripped his heart. But that knot made all his doubts disappear. "I will go and find her," he said.

"What about the children of the Northernmost Part of the World? They'll be left without a Lullaby Chanter."

"Sesi and Sila will sing for me. They are grey wolves, their howling is haunting, and they have ridden the sledge with me every night for as long as I can remember." Mumik looked at the grey wolves. "I know they don't have my voice. But the children worship their howling. Every child will continue to be comforted every night until I return." Mumik turned back to the White Bright Sprite. "I need your help. Can you tell me where is the Southernmost Part of the World?"

"It's at the bottom end of this world. All the way down south, a journey of many days," she answered.

"Well then, that's where I'll go," Mumik stated.

During supper, he told Koko all that had happened with his birthday wish. The Arctic fox listened, his front-facing ears alert to every word.

"I'll go with you," Koko said, and before Mumik could say anything, he added, "No, you won't change my mind. I'll be your first mate; I know a sailor-turned-igloo-maker who can lend us a boat."

Day One

In the Southernmost Part of the World

Pimnik Opipok closed her eyes, doubting she could ever do what she knew she must do. This was a strange feeling, for she was the most confident person the Southernmost Part of the World had ever seen. She never doubted any of her decisions. Ever. When a choice knocked at her door, she always knew what to do. But the decision before her was too big. So, for the first time since she could remember, a feeling of uncertainty built and grew inside her, making it very difficult to sleep.

Pimnik lived in a small snow house in the Southernmost Part of the World. A place of glaciers, frozen lakes and rivers of the clearest water. There was nothing but shades of white and icy blues. These were the most peaceful territories on Earth, and many believed they were so peaceful because no one dared disturb their beauty.

Pimnik had celebrated her twelfth birthday the day before. The morning had begun as usual:

she woke up, splashed cold water on her face and combed her waist-length hair into two braids. She made hot chocolate, ate a handful of blueberries and went outside. While she sipped hot chocolate, she used her fishing pole to scribble on the snow. That day's words were: Happy Birthday to Me. She practised a few lullabies on the harp and had lunch at the ice cream shop: two ice cream sandwiches, one lemon and one white chocolate. This was her tried and tested routine, and she rarely strayed from it.

Later in the day, she stopped by Aok and Oki's to return an ice pick she had borrowed the week before. Pimnik had met the pair of penguins one day when she needed a frozen carrot to decorate a snowman and they had happened to have one. Since then, a tradition had been born where if Pimnik needed something, she had only to knock on Aok and Oki's big snow house with its crooked chimney and they would lend it to her.

She knocked on their door, but no one answered.

She knocked again.

Nothing but silence.

Concerned that something might have happened, Pimnik opened the door and walked inside.

"Happy birthday!" Aok and Oki shouted, springing from behind a huge ice sculpture wearing birthday bonnets.

"Oh, thank you!" Pimnik said, genuinely surprised by her surprise party.

Aok gave Pimnik a birthday bonnet. Oki brought a cake made of frozen marshmallows, placed it on the table and lit the candles. When Pimnik was about to blow them out, Aok said, "Remember to ask for your birthday wish from the Peckish Pixie!"

Pimnik had not forgotten about the Peckish Pixie. She was a mischievous fairy of the south who granted your wishes if you left her a yummy treat near the Snarly Shrub, the tangled and knotty bush that was the Peckish Pixie's home. Pimnik closed her eyes tight. "Dear Peckish Pixie, I wish... I wish I weren't so very lonely," she whispered.

On her way home, she walked past the Snarly Shrub and left a slice of frozen marshmallow birthday cake under it. Then she ran to her snow house and climbed on her roof with her harp; warm in her hooded parka, she sang three long lullabies to the Southernmost Part of the World.

As soon as the sun went down each night, her lullabies were awaited with bated breath by every child of the Southernmost Part of the World. Sometimes they wished the day would pass quickly just to hear Pimnik's music. Her voice was silky and full of flavour, like the creamiest vanilla mousse. Yet her lullabies seemed to make everyone happy but her. The hollow sadness in Pimnik's heart would not leave, no matter how much she wished it away.

The next morning Pimnik woke up to a loud knock. She jumped out of bed and ran to the front door.

When she opened it, no one was there.

In front of her was a humongous box gift-wrapped with a blue ribbon tied in a bow. Stuck to it, there was a letter with her name on it.

She looked to the left. There was no one in sight.

She looked to the right. No one there either.

Pimnik put her morning routine on hold to open the letter and unwrap the box. She chose the letter first:

In this land of ice and white,
Your wish becomes my true delight.
When a dream is dreamt for long,
It becomes achingly strong.
Fear no more the lonely night,
Your twin brother shines a light.
A Lullaby Chanter he became,
Mumik Opipok is his name.
Your bond cannot be torn apart,
Fly North to mend your broken heart.

Snow Petrels will sing your lullabies each day,

And thus, your wish has found a way.

The Peckish Pixie

P.S. Thank you for the frozen marshmallow cake

"A brother!" Pimnik shouted. "A family at last! Thank you, Peckish Pixie!"

She moved on to the box, untying the blue ribbon as fast as she could.

"What is this?" Pimnik said, peering inside the box. There was a *really* big wicker basket, a huge coil of rope, some sort of burner and silky marigold-coloured fabric. She grabbed at a handbook that was wedged into one of the corners of the box. The title read: "Instructions for Building a Hot Air Balloon."

"Huh." Pimnik scratched her forehead, then leafed through the manual. "Let's get to work then."

It took her a while, but she managed to

build the whole thing before noon. Her ride to the Northernmost Part of the World was ready.

The most important rule of journey-planning, Pimnik thought, was to pack nourishing treats and, according to her, ice cream sandwiches fell into that category. So that was the first thing into the wicker basket. The second most important rule of journey-planning was easy: good music. That is what the harp was for. She also made a checklist and an inventory, because the third most important rule of journey-planning clearly stated: nothing must be left to chance.

Last but not least, Pimnik read about the essentials of balloon travel. As part of her gift, the Peckish Pixie had also put a compass into the wicker basket (so Pimnik would always know where north was). A map showed the dotted line that went from the Southernmost Part of the World to the Northernmost Part of the World (so she would know the fastest route).

That night Pimnik climbed on top of her roof with her harp. She stared at the star-filled sky and thought of Mumik. Then she sang her farewell lullabies.

Day Two

A Bit Farther Away From the Northernmost Part of the World

The sun had only just risen over the skyline, turning everything orangey white. Mumik and Koko had set sail a few hours ago. Their bearings: south. Very south. All the way to the bottom-of-the-world south.

Mumik stood behind the tiller. Koko looked at the charts, then over the bow, then at the charts again, then at the weather vane. He flattened his ears as he appraised the situation.

"I believe we are going in the right direction."

"Off we go to the Southernmost Part of the World!" Mumik said. He trimmed one of the sails just a little as the wind softened.

The sailboat cut across the choppy ocean. Mumik was fascinated by the way the boat bounced atop waves which softly crashed against the rusty hull.

"How long do you think it will take us to get there?" he asked Koko.

"Well," the Arctic fox replied, "if my calculations are right, we'll get there when we get there."

"That doesn't sound like a very precise calculation to me."

"They are philosophical calculations."

"But I want real calculations."

"Philosophical calculations are real calculations," Koko argued.

"But I'm looking for the exact number of days and hours," Mumik argued back.

"Why?" Koko asked.

"Because I can't wait to get there!" Mumik shouted, prancing around the boat.

"Aha," Koko looked at him with a cheeky grin.

"Oh, I see. Patience, right?" Mumik said.

"Right," Koko concurred.

Nothing was said for a while. They both kept silent, looking ahead, listening to the swish of the ocean.

Koko broke the silence. "What will be the first thing you say to Pimnik?"

"I've been thinking about that since the White Bright Sprite granted my wish. I think I will introduce myself first, but then I'm not sure...a handshake, maybe? I don't know... I don't know... or a hug? We are brother and sister after all, right? And then I will introduce you, of course," Mumik said.

"Thank you," Koko said, and, having appointed himself chef of the sailboat, he ducked into the cabin to prepare lunch.

Day Two

A Bit Farther Away From the Southernmost Part of the World

Pimnik Opipok awoke before dawn. She had barely slept and decided she wanted to see the sun come out from high up in the sky. She jumped into the wicker basket. The burner was fixed, up-oriented, to the basket. The flames of the burner inflated the silky marigold-coloured fabric into a big balloon that was connected to the wicker basket by the ropes. Everything was ready. Aok and Oki bit through the cords that held it to the ground and up she went.

"Bye, Oki! Bye, Aok!" she shouted as the balloon drifted upwards.

"Bye, Pimnik! Travel safe!" the penguins said in unison, waving their flippers in farewell.

The snow houses of the Southernmost Part of the World became smaller. When they had finally blurred into the snowy ground, Pimnik turned her gaze ahead. "Northernmost Part of the World, here

I come!" Her words echoed off the glaciers in the still, dark sky.

The balloon moved gently across clear skies. Gusts of wind rippled the ocean below, making the balloon speed up. The morning was chilly but not in an unfriendly way.

With the same burner that made the balloon fly, Pimnik heated some hot chocolate, and then she leant her elbows on the side of the basket as she watched the sun make its way up the sky. A few clouds in the distance were tinted a pinkish glow. The day was warming up.

Pimnik thought of Mumik. There were so many things she wanted to tell him: her favourite lullabies, her love for ice cream sandwiches, the wonders of the Southernmost Part of the World. The list was endless. Not to mention all the questions she wanted to ask him. She just knew they would talk for days.

Her train of thought was interrupted by the greeting of a wandering albatross.

"Hello there! How's it going?"

"Hey," Pimnik greeted back. "It's going well."

"I'm Albie," the wandering albatross said. He was a large, chiefly white, bird with narrow wings and a stern face. His name didn't quite match the seriousness of his look.

"Nice to meet you. I'm Pimnik Opipok."

"What an interesting device you're flying in."

"It's a hot air balloon."

"It's gigantic!"

"It is, isn't it? And you know what? My handbook said that it is one of the oldest forms of flying device used to carry people," Pimnik said proudly.

"But how do you make this huge thing float and fly?"

"It's simple," Pimnik said. "Hot air rises. I can float and fly in this huge thing by heating the air inside the balloon with this burner."

"Hmm, how remarkable. And I see you are heading north?"

"Yes, I'm going to the Northernmost Part of the World."

"I'm a bird of the southern oceans. I mainly wander these waters," Albie said, "but once or twice I have made my way to the north. A wonderful place, a land of white blizzards and magic tales. Quite special, enchanting if you will. But be careful with the thundershowers of the Tropical Circle; if you do, you will reach your destination before you know it."

"Thanks for the advice."

"Now, if you don't mind, I'm gonna go find myself some squid and krill for lunch."

"Good luck," Pimnik said, "and *bon appétit*."

"Good luck to you too, Pimnik Opipok," Albie said and he soared away.

Day Three

Nearing the Tropical Circle

So far, Mumik Opipok and Koko had learned three things about sailboats:

1) There is very little time to sleep. With a crew of two, one of them always had to be up, crewing the tiller and the sails, so they took turns to rest at night. Added to this was the never-ending sway of the boat. Not good.

2) A boat is an awfully small space. No matter how hard they tried, they were constantly bumping into each other.

3) But, when the wind billowed the sails, and the boat was almost flying over the white-crested waves, they felt a thrill unlike any other in their lives. It made up for too little sleep and the lack of space.

Mumik looked at the charts; they were

getting closer to the Tropical Circle. Gone were the days of frosty breezes, scarves and snow.

"It's so hot!" Koko said.

"What's wrong with the sun in this part of the world?" Mumik dried the sweat off his forehead.

"We're ill-prepared for this, Mumik."

They camped in the shadow the canopy from the main sail had cast on the deck.

"I like my cold weather." Mumik reminisced about the winters of the north, trying vainly to shrug off some of the wretched heat that seemed to be smothering him.

"Yep, I don't blend too well with this weather either," Koko said.

"I'm gonna get a bottle of cold water," Mumik said. "Do you want one?"

"Wow!" Koko said, his eyes wide open.

"What's the matter? Have we run out of water? I knew we should have brought more bottles!"

"No, no, we still have plenty."

"What is it then?" Mumik asked, squinting away from the sun and fanning himself with an old chart.

"Look at the colour of the sea!"

The ocean had turned from icy dark blue to crystal clear turquoise.

Mumik looked at the water. "And over there! Can you see that?"

A school of foreign-looking fish passed the sailboat, their shades of colours Mumik and Koko had never seen: fiery violet and pink, electric orange and the brightest shade of emerald green. As if hypnotised, Mumik and Koko stared at the fish.

"Forget the water," Mumik said, "I think I'm going in for a quick dip."

He had barely uttered the sentence when Koko threw the anchor overboard. As soon as the boat was secure, they jumped into the water. They laughed and splashed each other until they were exhausted, then let themselves float on their backs side by side.

"I take back what I said. I think I blend quite nicely here," Koko said. He talked about the many good things this new place had to offer until Mumik interrupted him.

"Um, I think we should get back to the sailboat."

"Why?"

"Over there. Look."

Koko turned to his left. A storm was brewing in the distance.

They hurried back to the boat and hoisted the sails. Koko weighed the anchor and Mumik grabbed the tiller. The wind blew harder.

"Which way?" Mumik asked Koko.

"That way," Koko said. He pointed to the storm.

"Are you serious? Right into the middle of that horrible thing?" Mumik shouted as thunder cracked overhead.

"The Southernmost Part of the World is that way. Look at the charts. There's no way around it!"

Without warning, heavy black clouds covered the sky. There was nothing left but darkness. The choppy waters had become angry waves that slammed into the boat. Ruthless storm winds tilted the sailboat madly from side to side. Koko tried to wrestle his way up the deck to ease up the main sail. Lightning flashed and lit up the entire sky. Mumik looked up.

"Did you see that? What was that?" Mumik asked.

"Lightning!"

"No, there's something in the sky, up there!" Mumik pointed upwards.

"I don't see anything," Koko said.

"Wait..."

A new bolt of lightning lit the sky for a few seconds.

"I saw it! It looks like a marigold-coloured hot air balloon! Seems like we're not the only ones trying to fight through this!" Koko said.

The sailboat was doing a good job of trying to fight the storm, but the storm kept fighting back, battering the rusty but sturdy vessel. Now the waves were as tall as the mast. A sense of doom came over Mumik.

"It's all part of the experience of being sailors!" Koko said bravely, ignoring the words of the former sailor-turned-igloo-maker, who had said that most sailors regard storms as the greatest danger on the water.

"I don't like this experience!"

"Should we turn back?" The wind grabbed Koko's words.

"What? I can't hear you!"

"Should we turn back?"

Mumik thought of Pimnik. His sense of doom vanished as his answer came straight to him. "Most definitely not!"

"Very well then, hold on tight!"

Day Three

In the Tropical Circle

Pimnik's days in the balloon went like this: take a whiff of fresh air to wake up. Check the compass to make sure she was heading north. Comb her waist-length hair and style it into braids. Heat some hot chocolate on the burner for breakfast. Discover new kinds of clouds. Clean the balloon (Pimnik was not a grime devotee). Practise the harp. Think about her arrival in the Northernmost Part of the World. She liked her new routine. At night, because there were no children in the sky, she sang her lullabies to the moon, who in Pimnik's opinion seemed to really like them.

As she got closer to the Tropical Circle, she made a slight change to her routine. The handbook had warned of the heat in this part of the world, so she had carefully prepared for it before leaving. The hot chocolate was switched for frozen lemonade. Following the third most important rule of journey-planning, *nothing must be left to chance*, she had also brought lighter clothes for the summery weather of the tropics.

Yet on the third day she saw the very thing the wandering albatross had warned her about. Stormy clouds began to roll in, their shadows swallowing the sun's rays. This was something for which she had not prepared. Thunder crackled and the rain began.

Pimnik made sure everything was tightly secured inside the balloon's basket, including herself.

While the wind slammed the rain relentlessly into her face, Pimnik made a mental list of her concerns:

1) Avoid falling through the fathomless abyss and into the ocean.
2) Hold on to the compass and make sure the balloon does not stray too much from the right course.
3) Try to stop the balloon from ripping itself apart.

She peeked out of the basket. The wind whipped her braids and threatened to tear them from her head as she looked to see if there was an island, or coastline, where she could land until the storm passed. There wasn't. Squinting through the gloom, it was clear: there was nothing but water all around her. She grabbed tighter to the rim of the basket. She had never seen such high waves before. They looked like giants capable of smashing up anything in their way.

Amidst the dips in those towering waves she spotted a little rusty sailboat swaying wildly, trying to stay afloat. "I hope that whoever's on that boat makes it to shore," she whispered, then she wished the same thing for herself. She knew they were both at the mercy of the winds. The balloon flailed on helplessly, making it almost impossible to steer forward.

When the balloon entered a rain cloud, everything turned dark grey. The thunder echoed so loudly Pimnik curled into a corner of the basket,

93

covered her ears and closed her eyes tight. This cloud was nothing like the fluffy white meringues she used to see in the skies of the Southernmost Part of the World. This cloud was a wrathful monster. Without opening her eyes, she began to sing a lullaby. The mad weather would decide her fate.

Day Four

Somewhere Closer to the Southernmost Part of the World

"That grumpy, miserable weather!" snapped Koko. "I'm telling you, that was no way to treat sailors!" The tropical storm was long gone but Mumik and Koko were still soaking wet, queasy and jittery. With a whirling sensation all over their bodies, they felt as if they had just come out of a washing machine. They were exhausted after teetering around the sailboat, trying to stay afloat.

Mumik was behind the tiller and Koko was inside the cabin; each was collecting his thoughts, together with everything that had flown about during the storm.

"I don't think the weather really cares about who's on the ocean when it decides to create a storm," Mumik said.

"Well, it *should* care!" Koko said, putting a plate and a cup back on the shelves.

"I'll tell you one thing I've learned from all this: the ocean can be a fearsome creature. I hope

I don't have to be in it when it gets angry again."

Koko came up to the cockpit with two tuna sandwiches. He gave one to Mumik and took a huge bite from his.

"OH Y–U–M!" Koko said, diving headfirst into the sandwich. "This is the best tuna sandwich I've had in my whole life!"

"Tell me about it. The best of the bestest," said Mumik, his mouth full.

"That's not a word," Koko said.

"I know, but I needed to stress how much I'm enjoying this sandwich right now, so I made it up."

"You can't just make up a word to highlight a thought."

"Why not?"

"Because you're not in charge of creating words. You don't make the rules for what words exist or not."

"Who does then?"

Koko pondered for a few seconds. "I don't really know, some sort of word committee, I guess."

"Well, I've never heard of any word committee and since we are alone in the middle of the ocean, I figure it's okay if I say the word *bestest* to convey my feelings about this awesome tuna sandwich."

"Fair enough," Koko conceded. "This sandwich is the best of the bestest then."

They finished their snack and shared a bottle of water.

Content and with full tummies, they sailed in silence for a long time. The sailboat bounced every now and then, spraying a cold mist over the deck. Whenever the wind shifted, Mumik fine-tuned the direction of the sailboat and Koko trimmed or eased the sails.

The weather began changing again. Chilly winds returned and the sun was not as warm as in the Tropical Circle. Mumik went into the cabin and brought back their coats, woollen gloves and winter socks.

Koko looked at the charts. "This cold means we're almost there, Mumik."

Goosebumps swirled all over Mumik's body and even though he tried to jiggle them away, they refused to leave. He had to say it out loud.

"I'm nervous, Koko."

The Arctic fox let go of the tiller for a moment and put a paw on his friend's back. "Everything will turn out alright, you'll see." As he said this, they both spotted in the horizon the white glaciers of the Southernmost Part of the World.

Day Four

Somewhere Closer to the Northernmost Part of the World

Pimnik was not sure how much time had passed but when she finished the lullaby and opened her eyes, the storm had cleared. The sky sported a few wisps of white clouds.

"So, this is what relief feels like," Pimnik said to herself, then sighed.

She made sure her harp was still there. It was, safe and in one piece. She looked at the compass and at the map. She had strayed from her destination a little but not too much. She resumed her journey north, slaloming through the clouds dotting the sky.

Pimnik discovered that tropical showers brought a wet, sticky smell and seriously frizzy hair. She untied her braids, combed her waist-grazing black hair to get rid of all snaggles and fuzziness, before re-braiding it neatly. While she did this, and out of the corner of her eyes, she saw that something was flying towards the balloon.

As it got closer, Pimnik realised it was a dunlin bird. It landed on the edge of the wicker basket. She stared at it. The bird stared back. It looked... *Worried* was the word that popped into Pimnik's head. The dunlin bird definitely looked upset.

"Are you okay?" Pimnik asked.

"No. I'm not," the bird answered. "I've lost my flock. I don't know what to do."

"How unfortunate." Pimnik was not really sure what to say.

"We dunlins always fly, feed and roost in flocks, and I've lost mine!" His voice broke as he choked back sobs. "I don't know how it happened. I must have been daydreaming. I am always daydreaming, and I know I shouldn't be, but I just can't help it." He thumped the side of the basket with a wing. "When I snapped back to reality, they were all gone! Argh! Why am I so feather-brained! How will I find them?"

"Would you like to stay with me?"

"But you're not a dunlin."

"No, I'm not. I'm Pimnik."

"I've never met a pimnik before."

"No, no, I'm not *a* pimnik. My name is Pimnik. There are no other Pimniks. There's only one of me."

"Huh… I guess there is only one of me too. I'm Mo."

"Do you know where your flock was heading, Mo?"

"I'm not sure. I usually fly at the back and I never really pay much attention. I think I heard them say we were heading north."

"Well, that's my bearing. I'm trying to reach the Northernmost Part of the World. Stay with me, if you want. We can keep each other company. And if we get some more wind, then we might even catch them up."

"Are you sure you don't mind?"

"The more the merrier, as they say."

"Okay then."

"Welcome aboard." She swept an arm around the wicker basket. "Make yourself at home."

The temperature dropped. The wintery weather was back. An icy breeze brushed in and cold seeped all the way down until it reached Pimnik's toes. She put on a woolly beanie and her hooded parka and heated up two mugs of hot chocolate, one for herself and one for Mo.

The balloon blew swiftly across the sky. Every now and then, Pimnik shot bursts of fire from the burner, so the balloon would stay high above the clouds. Hours rushed by as they talked about life and birds and lullabies and other assorted topics. Pimnik told Mo all about Mumik and the Peckish Pixie and her birthday wish. She also told him plenty about the Southernmost Part of the World, since Mo had never flown that far south.

Pimnik learned that dunlins are company-loving birds whose favourite dish is snails. Yuk, she thought, but she knew it would be rude to share this thought with her new friend.

There was a subtle shift in the sunlight as a pale-gold mid-afternoon set in. There were no clouds in the sky. There were no sounds either.

"What is it?" Mo asked when he saw that Pimnik had her eyes fixed in the distance.

"I think I see something," she answered without taking her eyes off the horizon. Mo looked to where Pimnik was looking.

"I don't see anything," he said.

"That blurry line up ahead."

"Is it a shore?"

Pimnik nodded. "I think we've made it, Mo... I think that's the Northernmost Part of the World."

Day Five

The Southernmost Part of the World

Gusts of bone-chilling wind told Mumik and Koko they had arrived at the Southernmost Part of the World. They moored the sailboat in a narrow quay and walked to the nearby village. Everything was covered in snow, just like in the Northernmost Part of the World.

The village was made up of a cluster of small snow houses, an ice cream shop, and a main road lined with pine trees. A special kind of charm drizzled over the place like hot chocolate. A handful of people were moseying around but other than that the place seemed to live in complete stillness.

Mumik was getting antsy and before he knew it, he was asking a passer-by if he knew where Pimnik Opipok lived.

"Our great Lullaby Chanter, of course, she lives in that last house over there, but..."

"But what?" Mumik asked, just about stopping himself from screaming it at the passer-by.

"Ask Aok and Oki, they live in the big snow house with the crooked chimney." The passer-by pointed to the house on the edge of the village.

"Thank you," said Mumik as he and Koko darted away towards Aok and Oki's snow house.

After five uninterrupted knocks, Oki opened the door.

"Are you Aok or Oki?" Mumik asked.

"I'm Oki."

"My name is Mumik Opipok."

"Oh…" Oki gasped. He didn't need an explanation to grasp the conundrum. Once he invited Mumik and Koko inside, they in turn told Aok and Oki about their journey south.

"That same day, the day of your birthday, Pimnik found out about you as well and off she went to look for you. She left the next day for the Northernmost Part of the World in a hot air balloon the Peckish Pixie gave her," said Aok.

Mumik and Koko looked at each other and knew at once it was Pimnik who they had seen during the storms in the Tropical Circle.

"We need to hurry home, Koko. We need to get there before she leaves!" Mumik said.

"But what if she's already gone by the time we get there, maybe the wisest choice is to stay here and wait for her to come back," Koko said.

"What if she doesn't come back?"

"I think going back is too risky, Mumik," the Arctic fox said.

"What does your heart tell you?" Aok asked Mumik. "What do you *feel* you should do?"

Mumik closed his eyes. "I can't wait. We have to sail back home, Koko," he said at last, "even if it's too late by the time we get there."

Day Five
The Northernmost Part of the World

As they floated above the shore of the Northernmost Part of the World, Pimnik and Mo suddenly heard a high-pitched scratchy sound. It was coming from behind. They turned sharply.

Ooooooh!

Ooooooh!

Ooooooh!

"I can't really make it out," Mo said.

"I can't either," Pimnik said.

The sound grew louder.

"Wait... Listen closely," Pimnik said.

They squinted their eyes and pointed their ears towards the sound.

Moooooooh!

Moooooooh!

Moooooooh!

As the sound became clearer, a flock of dunlin birds became visible in the distance, twisting and banking in unison, displaying impressive aerial manoeuvres.

"Pimnik, it's them!" Mo said proudly.

"Go! Go to your family!" she told him.

"Thank you for the ride, Pimnik Opipok."

"Any time."

They waited until the flock caught up with them and Mo leapt off the side of the wicker basket to join them. Pimnik vaguely heard them berating Mo as the balloon flew on and Mo continued his journey with his flock.

In order to land in the Northernmost Part of the World, Pimnik had to allow the air inside the balloon to cool. And so, the not-so-hot air balloon slowly began to drift down until it landed.

Everything was snowy, silvery white and spotless. "So much like home," she said to herself.

There was nothing but an ash tree that had stalactites instead of branches and snowflakes instead of leaves. Standing on one of the stalactites, Pimnik spotted a dazzling tiny creature.

"Welcome to the Ivory Ash. I'm the White Bright Sprite."

"Hello. I have just arrived from the Southernmost Part of the World. I'm looking for Mumik Opipok. My name is—"

"Pimnik Opipok," the White Bright Sprite said.

"How do you know who I am?" Pimnik asked.

"You have the same big black eyes as your brother and you both have the same smile, a smile with the right amount of wit," the White Bright Sprite answered.

"You know Mumik?"

"I do, yes."

"Do you know where I can find him?"

The White Bright Sprite told Pimnik about Mumik's birthday wish and his journey to the Southernmost Part of the World.

Pimnik's mouth twitched as she fought her tears. She won the fight but her dark eyes were still lit with sadness.

"Such a long journey," she whispered and knelt down on the snow, "such a long wait."

"It's okay to be sad, or mad, or both if you want," the White Bright Sprite said.

Pimnik didn't say anything. She was still kneeling, staring at the snow.

"But you can't lose your strength, Pimnik Opipok," the White Bright Sprite said.

"I don't..." Pimnik started but couldn't finish the sentence.

"I know," the White Bright Sprite said. "It seems too hard not to, but I believe you can do it."

Pimnik looked up at the White Bright Sprite. She stood up and took a deep breath.

"You're right. If a round trip to the south is what it takes, then that is what I will do. I'll have to fly faster though; I have to get there before Mumik leaves."

Day Six

A Bit Farther Away From the Southernmost Part of the World

The journey back to the Northernmost Part of the World began as a harrowing experience. If only Mumik could break the rules of time and be back home in the blink of an eye. But he knew he couldn't. He had to abide by what the winds and the tides allowed.

It was not easy. As Koko had told him at the beginning of the trip, he had to be patient but he just felt acutely flustered. To take his mind off things, he tried to bake a fish soufflé for supper, but he was so upset by the whole situation, the soufflé came out flat and soggy instead of tall and puffy.

While they ate the deflated soufflé, Koko did his best to cheer Mumik up. "We have to see the challenges for what they truly are: a gift!"

"A gift? What are you talking about?"

Koko realised this was not going to be simple. "I'm just saying, the obstacles we found on our journey were there to teach us something. Don't you think?"

"No, I don't." Mumik did not really feel like looking at the bright and happy side of life.

Koko ignored that and pressed on. "I'm telling you, every problem is a test and no matter if we excel or fail, it will always teach us something about ourselves."

"Koko, I'm not in the mood for your philosophical views of existence. I'm too sad right now."

"But this was just a little setback."

"Little?"

"Okay, maybe you're right, it wasn't a *little* setback. It was a big one. But it is still only a setback. See it for what it truly is."

"But what if I never meet Pimnik."

"Oh, boy! You are good at embellishing an ugly thought with even uglier thoughts. This isn't the end!"

"It isn't?"

"Of course it isn't."

Mumik took a moment to consider. "Fine. I'll try to stop piling on ugly thoughts."

"That's what I'm talking about. I'm going to do the dishes now. We'll be in the Tropical Circle tomorrow and we'll have arrived home before we know it."

Day Six

A Bit Farther Away From the Northernmost Part of the World

The balloon was flying at full speed to the Southernmost Part of the World. Pimnik didn't take her eyes off the skyline. She felt the balloon would slow down if she did. To her right, the sun was setting, but she barely noticed. She was so focused on her destination, she hardly blinked, that is until her eyes started watering to let her know they were in desperate need of a wink at least. She closed her eyes slowly and dried the tears off her face.

A full moon loomed out of the darkness. Pimnik could not help but wish she had made the right decision. It was hard to shake off the worry. Would the future prove to be surprising in a good way? She did not know, and she hated not knowing.

She saw her harp and thought about singing a lullaby to the moon. Would time pass by quicker?

It did not matter. She really didn't feel like it. "I'm sorry, moon, not today. Maybe tomorrow."

She heated up some hot chocolate and remembered how she used to scribble words in the snow. If she could scribble something now to describe how she felt, it would be: Discombobulated. Terribly baffled and utterly confused.

With the moon floating beside her, Pimnik snuggled down under her blanket in the corner of the basket and fell asleep.

Day Seven
Nearing the Tropical Circle Once More

Mumik and Koko found themselves in the middle of a fiery discussion. Mumik was holding the tiller but wasn't really paying attention to where the sailboat was going. Koko was throwing his paws in the air to make his case with extra oomph.

"It's boiling hot, Mumik! And look at that clear, cool water!"

"We don't have time for this, Koko!"

"I know we're in a rush, but it would only be a quick dip!"

"Don't even think about it!"

"I'll jump in and out."

"We should take advantage of the fact that there are no storms in sight. Do you want to go through that again?"

"A storm won't appear out of the blue in five minutes. Please, Mumik, I'm melting!"

"Then grab some seawater with that bucket and freshen up."

"Pfff! A bucket? Really?"

"Every second counts, Koko. We can't risk missing Pimnik again!"

A loud, smashing sound coming from the bow of the sailboat cut off Mumik and Koko's discussion.

"What in the world was that?" Koko jumped up. Mumik looked ahead and gasped.

They both bolted towards the bow of the boat.

Day Seven

Nearing the Tropical Circle Once More

Dawn broke in the Tropical Circle and the first rays of sunshine bathed the balloon in warmth. Pimnik was woken by an obnoxious, steady flapping noise. It sounded like a flag whipping in the wind. *But there are no flags here*, Pimnik thought. She hadn't even opened her eyes yet. She rubbed at them tiredly and when she eventually opened them, she saw a toucan was circling the balloon.

The toucan had black plumage, bright red feathers under his tail and a ginormous light-green banana-shaped beak, which was so big, it was almost the size of his entire body.

"Good morning," Pimnik said, but the toucan did not answer. He did not even glance at her. He was gaping at the balloon while orbiting around it. He seemed mesmerised. He kept flapping his wings in the most vexing manner and smacking his colourful beak.

"Oh, what a breakfast feast!" the toucan

said, not to Pimnik but to himself.

It suddenly dawned on Pimnik that the toucan probably thought the balloon was some sort of giant pear, or mango, or peach. The toucan flew to the top of the balloon and landed on it. He stood, rooted to the spot, still smacking his colourful beak.

"Excuse me!" Pimnik shouted. "This isn't a fruit! It's a balloon! Please don't peck it! You can't eat it!"

The toucan did not seem to be listening to her. He was drooling over his soon-to-be-devoured balloon-fruit.

"Excuse me!" Pimnik tried again. "Did you hear me? Don't peck…"

Too late.

The toucan had discovered it wasn't a giant pear, or mango, or peach. Frightened out of its wits by the hissing hot air coming out of the balloon, the toucan had flown away. Pimnik was left with a shrinking, descending balloon.

Luckily, the hole the toucan had made was not too big, so the air leaked slowly. The balloon did not plummet from the sky like a torpedo. It whirled down almost like a rose petal. Pimnik knew that soon she would fall into the ocean. A shrunken balloon (or a good one, for that matter) would not do much good here. She needed to find a place to land.

The balloon kept falling. As it fell, Pimnik scoured the ocean to see if there was anywhere she could try to land. She spotted a rusty sailboat and tried to steer her way towards it. As she got closer, she held tightly to the rim of the basket and closed her eyes.

"Here we go!" she whispered and did her best to cushion the blow.

A loud, smashing sound coming from the bow of the sailboat cut off Mumik and Koko's discussion about a possible dip in the ocean.

"What in the world was that?" Koko jumped up. Mumik looked ahead and gasped.

They both bolted towards the bow of the boat where they found a shrunken hot air balloon and a wicker basket attached to it.

"Is that…?" Mumik asked.

"I think it is," Koko answered.

From the basket, a discombobulated girl popped her head out. She had big black eyes, long black hair crafted into two waist-length braids and a very familiar smile.

"Pimnik?" Mumik asked.

Pimnik looked at the boy standing in front of her. She was quite wobbly, but she knew it was him the moment she saw him.

"Mumik!"

They looked at each other and smiled the same smile, a smile with the right amount of wit. For a moment nobody said anything, not even Koko. Then Mumik ran towards Pimnik and Pimnik sprinted to meet him.

They would never forget that day in the Tropical Circle. The day they found each other.

Epilogue

Mumik and Pimnik became a lullaby duet, singing songs together for both the Northernmost Part of the World and the Southernmost Part of the World.

They lived half of the eternal winter in the north and half of it in the south. They travelled either by rusty sailboat or by patched hot air balloon, but *always* avoiding tropical storms.

When they were in the south, Sesi and Sila howled the lullabies for them in the Northernmost Part of the World, and when they were in the north, the snow petrels filled in for them in the Southernmost Part of the World.

If they were in the south, they climbed to the top of Pimnik's snow house to chant their songs. If they were in the north, they sang while riding on Mumik's sledge.

Every day at twilight, Mumik and Pimnik's lullabies were heard around the world and every child fell asleep swiftly and dreamt good dreams.

Neboo McCloudy

High up in the skies there was a place called Floccusville. Hidden from all corners of the universe, it remained invisible to even the most powerful telescopes. It was a hamlet made of clouds, where hope floated, time flew and thoughts whizzed.

In this otherworldly world, clouds came in every shape. Some were old, small and wispy. Some were new, big and spongy. A few were as tall as castle towers and others were as swollen as mushrooms. But no matter their shape, they all drifted lazily across the sky.

All the clouds in Floccusville were white. All except one. A stormy grey cloud that was home to Neboo McCloudy.

Like all the creatures of Floccusville, Neboo had big eyes, pinkish chubby cheeks and droopy ears. But one feature really singled him out: his droopy ears turned into pointy devilish spikes whenever he became too annoyed, which happened often.

Being a seasoned slugabed, whose days were filled with idle hours, Neboo found guiltless delight

in taking long naps. When he travelled around Floccusville, it was in an old-fashioned paraglider with a little propeller thrumming at the back. These trips around the clouds were the height of his days. For Neboo, it was the splendour of the ride that mattered, not the journey's end.

Like any other morning, Neboo woke up grumbling instead of yawning; he had a cup of extra-strong black coffee, no sugar, no cream. He put on his velvety bluish-grey jumpsuit with a hoodie. This was his only attire. He actually had two of these outfits; both were identical. He wore one when he had to wash the other and vice versa. He liked to keep things simple. Anything that had to do with household chores was, to the best of his knowledge, a waste of time. So, the less time he spent on them the better.

All set, he strapped on his paraglider, powered the little propeller and left his cloud for a morning ride. He made a first stop at the Market of Buttery Baked Buns. Inside, he found over a dozen other customers waiting in line. The raucous sound of everyone laughing and chatting made his droopy ears spring up into pointy devilish spikes.

"OH, FOR CRYING OUT LOUD!" Neboo yelled. The heads of everyone in the market jerked around, but Neboo was already speeding away, dangling from his glider.

"What can you expect of Neboo McCloudy?" one of the customers said.

"Come what may, he sticks to his unsavoury behaviour like gooey old marmalade," the owner of the market added. "It's as if he's happier when he's unhappy."

People often wondered why he was such a cranky fellow. Was it in his nature? Some said it was just that he was who he was. It was etched in his very essence. Others believed he had become so used to being grumpy that he neither knew nor cared about being anything different. But no one knew the truth. And no one dared ask him, either out of fear of getting yelled at or to avert an ugly bicker.

Neboo flew above the Park of Bougainvillea Billows, a seemingly never-ending garden with meadows of sweet-scented yellow flowers where everyone in Floccusville went on breezy mornings and sunny afternoons. It was quite early in the day and the air was chilly. Neboo was about to utter a surly remark about the temperature when something caught his attention. Further ahead, right above a small raggedy cloud, a scroll of paper glided.

He sped up to catch it before anybody else could. But even when he stretched his arm, he couldn't reach it. A sudden blast of wind took the scroll away. Neboo manoeuvred the paraglider and made a sharp turn to the left. He tried again as the scroll flailed this way and that. There was a third attempt, when he managed to hold it for *one* split second before it slipped through his hand. Then came his fourth effort. The scroll whizzed by him and disappeared inside a cloud. Neboo dived inside after it, waving his arms around to find the roll of parchment. He struggled through the brume and dimness until after one final gruelling stretch, he snatched it. Victory was his!

Scroll in possession, he jetted to a little lonely cloud, turned off the propeller and unstrapped his glider. He mopped sulky beads of sweat from his forehead and caught his breath. In uncharacteristic excitement, he hopped around. His hands worked unbelievably fast to unroll the scroll.

The note read:

In the skies of Oraland,
Endless fortune is at hand;
The Great Treasure will appear,
If you're smart enough to hear:
You will find the magic key
Inside a clover oozing glee.
If you don't see and you are not,
You will untie the guardian's knot.

"Oh, yes, yes, yes! I want The Great Treasure!" he said aloud, almost yodelling. His greedy side overpowered his lazy side. The journey's end had become important: a quest was the only way to get there.

He looked around to make sure no one had seen the rolled parchment. Relieved to be alone, he returned to his home cloud to prepare things for his journey. Having never journeyed outside of Floccusville, he wasn't sure what to pack. He pondered before deciding that the smartest way to travel was to travel lightly: a bottle of rainwater, a jar of marshmallows and his matching featherlike cream scarf and gloves, in case it got cold. Zipping everything into his rucksack, he stepped off his grey cloud.

Neboo had heard of Oraland, but he didn't know the exact way. What he did know was that he would have to go east, past the Caramel Way, a quiet place in the skies where all the carrier pigeons rested and catnapped on long journeys. After that, well, he would worry about that later.

He travelled speedily through the vast sky. A day passed before his startled eyes witnessed one shooting star chasing another through the clear, dark airspace. They glowed so brightly, he had to cover his eyes as they whizzed past him. He discovered by squinting his eyes that all the stars joined up like a dot-to-dot, creating the funniest-shaped squiggles.

After the third day, Neboo pulled up at a big sign that read: "Bubbleton, the Village of Bubble Makers".

A peculiar little gentleman – who looked like he was made out of balloons – was standing near the sign. He had a big smile and he spoke cheerfully to Neboo: "Welcome, sir! You have arrived at the Floating Village of Bubbleton. Please, come into our world."

Neboo didn't say anything back – and he certainly didn't smile back – but he did as he was asked.

A very particular sound surrounded him as soon as he stepped inside Bubbleton.

BSHHHHHHHHHH!!!

It was like stepping into a can of sugary soda. This was indeed the frothiest place Neboo had ever seen. Bubbles, bubbles and more bubbles everywhere. All transparent. All fizzy. Everything bouncy.

Neboo stared blankly at all the Bubbletonians. They were all smiling. Yep: every single one of them. Either smiling, giggling, laughing or grinning. Everyone glided gleefully among the soapy glistening bubbles. Some bubbles were so big, the baby Bubbletonians could get inside, roll around and probably see the town all wobbly and iridescent.

Everything in Bubbleton was happy, airy and cute. Neboo's droopy ears had turned into pointy devilish spikes. His neck was sweaty, his stomach was turning upside down, and his pinkish chubby cheeks swelled up and got chubbier to the point of explosion. The classic symptoms of witnessing what he could only describe as A Revolting Sight Extraordinaire.

He thought of words like "Yuk" and "Eww" but they weren't disgusting enough. "PWWWAJ!" he finally hurled. "What is the matter with the people in this village? This is even worse than Floccusville!"

Out of the corner of his eye, he saw a group of Bubbletonian kids floating towards him in big fat bubbles. Neboo pretended not to see them. He thought of slyly popping their bubbles just to ruin their fun but then decided that it was better to dash away as fast as he could. He had three main reasons for doing this:

1) He hated this merry place.
2) He was not fond of talking to anyone, especially children, and most especially happy children.
3) He did not want to be asked where he was going and be forced to reveal to these strangers his secret about The Great Treasure. There was no way he was going to share *that* with anyone.

Before someone else attempted to get close to him, he scurried out of Bubbleton; almost knocking the smile from the jolly gentleman standing at the entrance, Neboo journeyed on.

He flew east for hours, hearing nothing but the hissing of air.

"Argh! I'm so bored!" Neboo had become so fed up with the weary ride, he was now talking to himself. "Bored, bored, bored, I'll tell you! You'll tell me? Yes, I'll tell you. I'll tell you now, this stinks. It stinks worse than lavender, or roses, or any of those flowery smells! Where's the Caramel Way? I wanna get there already! What is there to do here? Think, Neboo, think!"

So, he thought. He thought until an idea popped into his head. When that happened, he smirked in triumph. "Lists!" He was good with lists.

To dust off his boredom, Neboo McCloudy began naming his favourite words.

The first word was easy. It belonged to the word NO.

The list went on:

Snot

Abominable

Mouldy

Grisly

Sour

Petulant

Grovel

Pudgy

Mole

Oaf

Mucky

Fester

"Useless! This isn't helping, I feel worse than before," he mumbled. Too fed up for once to be cheered by word lists, he got lost in his own boredom again.

Yet even as he was getting really tired and his level of crankiness was reaching its peak, he spotted something in the distance: curls of smoky, reddish-yellow mist and trails of light haze rested on the horizon. Neboo picked up the scent of syrupy tangerines and sugary peaches. He had arrived at the Caramel Way.

"OUT OF MY WAY, BIRDS!!!" Neboo shouted at a flock of carrier pigeons that were flying pleasantly in perfect formation.

"So sorry, sir!" they cooed, but Neboo was already speeding away from them.

Later, sitting on a mushy cloud, he took a deep breath of relief, refreshed himself with some rainwater from his bottle, opened his jar and ate some marshmallows.

The snack improved his mood, but only lasted a brief moment. He remembered he didn't know where to go from here, and he quickly grew mad, angry, impatient and all manner of other annoyed feelings. His droopy ears were about to turn into pointy devilish spikes when something interrupted his spiralling grouchiness.

"Are you okay there, sir?"

Neboo looked up and saw a lonesome carrier pigeon, with aviator goggles and a messenger bag across its chest, hovering on the orangey mist. A frown settled on Neboo's face. He was quite talented when it came to doing nasty facial expressions: a frown, a scowl, a grimace, a sneer. He was a master of them all, even the eye-rolling and headshaking.

"I'm tired and lost!" Neboo barked.

"Where do you need to go?" the carrier pigeon cooed placidly.

Neboo found himself in an awkward situation. He didn't want to share his precious destination with anyone, but he also needed help to journey on. It took him a while to answer.

"To Oraland," he said through clenched teeth. He could feel his droopy ears stretching upwards.

"A very mystical place, deeply secret, or so I've heard. Why would you want to go there?"

"I have my reasons, which I don't plan to tell you." Neboo snarled, flustered by the fact that he had needed to ask for a favour and because deep down he was hoping the carrier pigeon would tell him the way.

"Fair enough, sir. There's no need to share your reasons," the pigeon said kindly. "Oraland is almost at the end of this universe. It's a place at the border. There you will find the wise clouds that sleep at the edge of the sky. I've never been there myself but that's pretty much how the legend goes."

"Legend?"

"Figure of speech. I don't know anyone who's actually been there. I've only heard stories from carrier pigeons who've heard stories from other carrier pigeons. Be that as it may, this is what I can tell you: keep flying east, along the Rainbow Path, until you see the big nimbus cloud called Efflo, where Babette and Bernard, the artful bakers, live. After that, you should head north. But, I'm sad to say, that's as far as I was told. What lies ahead of that,

I do not know. Babette and Bernard might have more information. Good luck to you, sir!" The bird soared with the greatest of ease, away from Neboo.

Neboo was left with a prickly feeling all over his body, but he didn't know exactly why. He didn't care to wallow in it though. He had the answer he wanted.

Neboo did as the carrier pigeon instructed. He kept flying east. He crossed the Rainbow Path, a multicoloured arch, glossy and clear in the morning light. After seven or eight yawns in a row, he decided to get some rest. He put his glider on autopilot, set it for east and, before he knew it, he was fast asleep.

The first thing he saw when he woke up was a big white cloud shaped like a cauliflower.

When Neboo flew near it, a well-rounded fellow with a long white chef's hat waved his hand with a welcoming gesture.

Neboo's first instinct was to reject the invitation. His lips tightened as he remembered Bubbleton.

He thought it best to ignore the man and stay focused on the treasure. But then again, he was a bit intrigued and a bit tired and the smell of chocolate wafting from the cloud was the best enticement he needed to change his mind and accept the invitation.

"Hello there!" the man said.

"Hello," Neboo said.

"I'm Bernard, the artful baker. Welcome to Efflo!"

"Oh, so you're Bernard. A carrier pigeon told me about you."

"Did he happen to tell you that I'm a pastry cook renowned for the spongiest lemon soufflés, the fluffiest strawberry cupcakes and the most scrumptious chocolate mousse?"

"No, he didn't." Neboo's stomach growled as loud as a lion. He had been surviving on marshmallows and rainwater for days and the sound of this glorious food seemed like a miracle.

"Creatures from all over the skies come to Efflo to try my mouth-watering treats."

A lady appeared from the other end of the cloud. "This is my wife, Babette. She's also a *pâtissier*," Bernard said. "She's famous for her violet cotton candy."

"Hello, my name is Neboo McCloudy, I come from Floccusville."

"Never been. Nice?" Babette asked. Then she neatened her curly locks and arranged her cooking apron.

"I guess," Neboo answered flatly.

"You don't sound too convinced."

"No, no, it is."

"What is it?"

"Nice. Floccusville."

"Right. Why?"

"I don't know. It's cloudy."

"And where are you heading, might I ask?"

"To Oraland," Neboo answered. Sharing this piece of information came easier this time around.

"That is a long journey," Bernard said. "You must be hungry. What would you like? Perhaps lemon soufflés? Or chocolate mousse? We also have strawberry cupcakes straight out of the cloud-stove." The baker propped up a tray with all the things he had mentioned.

"Everything looks so good," Neboo confessed, not taking his eyes off the food.

"Then have a bit of everything!" Bernard said, handing Neboo a freshly baked cupcake.

"Thank you." These two words just slipped out of Neboo; saying them felt strange, almost as if he was speaking a foreign language.

"Are you sure you want to go to Oraland?" Babette asked.

"Yes, why?" Neboo asked through a mouthful of cupcake. It tasted like strawberries and buttercream, but it also tasted like magic, beauty and excitement.

"Well, the forest…" Babette answered.

"What forest?" Neboo asked.

"To get to Oraland, you have to go through the Formidable Forest of Foam," Babette answered.

"Oh…" Neboo whispered as he accepted another cupcake.

"You must be careful," Babette said. "They say its trees ooze a greenish foam. If you touch it, you'll be glued to the tree forever."

"Oh…" Neboo whispered again. His throat closed up and refused to allow him to swallow even the tiniest morsel of the strawberry cupcake, delicious as it was.

"Babette, don't frighten the poor fella," Bernard said. "I'm sure it's not that bad, it's just a forest."

"A formidable one," Neboo said.

"Try this. I promise it will make you feel better." Bernard handed Neboo a bowl of chocolate mousse and a big spoon.

Although he had lost his appetite for cupcakes after what he had just heard, Neboo accepted the bowl: the mousse looked too succulent not to.

His appetite immediately recovered when he tasted the chocolate mousse. It was the yummiest thing Neboo had ever eaten: creamy, nutty, silky and in all respects finger-licking and lip-smackingly perfect.

"Do you know which way I have to travel to get there?" he asked the bakers, after gulping down the last spoonful of mousse.

Bernard and Babette told Neboo that if he wanted to get to Oraland, he would have to fly north. Neboo listened carefully while feasting on a refilled bowl of chocolate mousse.

"You'll have to travel across many clouds before you reach the Formidable Forest of Foam, but keep these bearings and you should get there in a few days. If you find your way through the forest, you should arrive at Oraland," Babette said.

"*Should*?" Neboo asked.

"Well, we've actually never gone that far. Nor has anyone we know," Bernard said.

"I see. I keep hearing that."

"Hope you find what you're looking for," Babette said.

"Me too," Neboo said.

"We wish you safe travels, Neboo McCloudy," Bernard and Babette said in unison.

Neboo finished his cupcake and the mousse. With a warm feeling in his tummy, he said *thank you* one more time. He powered up the propeller and left Efflo, heading north.

That night, the chill of the evening blew in frolicking breezy waves. Neboo kept warm with his fluffy featherlike scarf and gloves. When it got dark, he saw that the moon was not hovering over him. It was right beside him, lighting his way and keeping guard over his journey.

He saw three sunrises and three twilights before he caught sight of a long and feline-shaped cloud. "This cannot be the Formidable Forest of Foam," Neboo said to himself. It was almost dusk. The sky had shifted from twinkle-toed turquoise to dark blue, and this catlike cloud looked spellbinding. For a second, Neboo thought he heard its deep, echoing purr.

"Greetings, Neboo McCloudy, welcome to Ocelotte," said an odd-looking little man standing on the cloud.

"How do you know who I am?" Neboo asked, taken aback.

"I know your name but I don't know who you are," the odd-looking little man answered. He wore a white turban and an indigo robe; he had freckles on his cheeks and was puffing scented smoke from a sandalwood pipe.

"How do you know my name?" Neboo asked.

"I know many things but many others I ignore," the odd-looking little man answered. "For instance, I don't know why you are visiting this part of the universe."

"I'm heading to the Formidable Forest of Foam. I'm actually trying to get to Oraland but I've been told I have to go through that forest first."

"Few people dare enter the Formidable Forest of Foam. It's formidably foamy, with the ever-burning flames above and the ever-blowing blizzards below."

"I'm brave."

"Indeed you are, Neboo McCloudy, and that's a good thing to be. Magnificent things happen to bold creatures who dare go where others don't," the odd-looking little man said. His voice sounded as if nothing could trouble him.

Neboo wasn't sure what to say next. Who was this weird-looking man with that funny hat and those extravagant sayings? Neboo stared at him as if trying to solve an unsolvable puzzle.

"What else are you?" the little man asked.

"Why do you ask so many questions?" Neboo asked back, half seriously cranky, half genuinely intrigued.

"You asked the first one. I just answered and continued our conversation. I like conversations. I don't have them very often. I'm usually alone in this part of the universe and sometimes I get bored."

"I'm always alone but I'm not bored," Neboo lied.

"Are you sure?"

There was no witty comeback. Neboo remained doubtfully silent.

"Are you all right, Neboo McCloudy?"

"Who are you?"

"I'm me. I'm Alphonse, the alchemist."

"The *what*?"

"An alchemist is a person who studies the art of changing something common into something special. I practise the art of amazing transformations."

"Sounds strange," Neboo stated, narrowing his eyes.

Alphonse drew on his sandalwood pipe and blew out a perfect circle of smoke. As the circle frayed around the edges, then dissipated, he put his hand inside his cloud and pulled out an old sackcloth, a jar with a glowing purple liquid and what Neboo reckoned to be the strangest device he'd ever seen. It was a mix between a pair of compasses, a pair of scissors and a pair of spectacles. With it, Alphonse cut a big triangle out of the sackcloth. He sprinkled the triangle with the glowing purple liquid. The drops spread and a dewy light started to swirl around the cloth. It covered the whole triangle and then slowly faded, revealing a fluffy featherlike creamy cape.

"To match the scarf and gloves you're wearing," Alphonse said.

"Oh…" Neboo's eyebrows rose. His big eyes did not blink and were lit in amazement.

"Everything in life can be transformed for the better," Alphonse said.

Neboo was feeling a bit more comfortable. This was probably the longest conversation he had had in all his life and it was the first time someone had ever given him a present. A present. A thing given to someone as a gift. A thing given *willingly* to someone without wanting anything in return.

Neboo let his guard down for a second and asked almost kindly, "You were right before, I do need to pass through the Formidable Forest of Foam. Do you know how I can do that?"

"To reach your destiny, you simply have to ask the right questions."

Just when I was beginning to like this odd-looking little man, Neboo thought. He wanted to hurl a nasty barb at him. But he refrained, took a deep breath and counted...

One...

Two...

Three...

Instead of behaving as he normally would – rude, mean and pompous – Neboo thought about what Alphonse had said to him.

"I can't fly over it on my paraglider, can I?"

"No, you cannot. As I said, above the forest dwell the ever-burning flames and below it the ever-blowing blizzards."

"Has anybody made it to the other side?"

"The answer to that question is not important."

"Do I need something to get to the other side?"

"Yes, you do."

"Would you help me?"

"Of course, it will be my pleasure." Alphonse stuck his hand inside Ocelotte once again and rummaged around till he found what he was looking for. "Here, take these gifts, they are for you. With them, you'll find your way through the Formidable Forest of Foam."

Alphonse gave Neboo three little bags, each with a tag stitched to it. On each tag there was a number and two words:

#1 – The Light

#2 – The Way

#3 – The Changes

"What are these? What's in them? Can I open them now? What are they for?"

"The answer to some questions must be found

only by he who has asked them."

"But how will I know when to use them? Or how?"

"How do you know when you are feeling troubled about something?"

"Well, I just know."

"There you go."

Neboo felt a bit iffy about the whole matter but he figured he didn't have much option other than to trust the alchemist. He put the three little bags in his rucksack. As he was getting ready to leave, Alphonse turned to him. "Don't forget your cape, Neboo, and never lose sight of the things that truly matter."

"What are those things?"

"I told you…"

"Right: *the answer to some questions must be found only by he who's asked them*. But why?"

"Because if I told you, you would never see why they truly matter."

For the first time ever, Neboo McCloudy

extended his hand in farewell. Alphonse smiled and shook Neboo's hand. They said goodbye and, fully prepared and equipped, Neboo McCloudy left Ocelotte and headed to the Formidable Forest of Foam.

Neboo had rolled up the parachute of the glider and collapsed the little propeller. He folded everything neatly into his rucksack and crossed the threshold of the forest with small but firm steps. Once inside, the ground felt cold. *Probably the ever-blowing blizzards below*, he thought.

Inside the Formidable Forest of Foam, the ground was squishy. It was like walking on a bunch of grapes. It was dark, muggy and gloomy.

Gradually, Neboo's eyes adjusted to the darkness. Only a little bit though, just enough to get a glimpse of the tall and pulpy trees. Their leaves looked spumy. Most of the trunks and branches were lathered with the greenish foam Bernard and Babette had mentioned. Here and there, billows of foam glided down to the ground and stuck to one another, becoming whipped shrubs that oozed the rottenest smell. High-reaching sudsy-like bows twined together covering the sky. The ever-burning flames were hidden above this wild, thick roof.

It was difficult to walk. Neboo dodged the foamy shrubs as best he could and avoided touching any of the trees, but it wasn't easy. It was still a heavily unlit territory. He couldn't see much and didn't know which way to go. Worst of all, there were no trails to follow.

There was not a single sound. There were clearly no animals or creatures living there. Neboo wasn't sure if this was a good thing or an eerie omen. His gut told him that the latter seemed more appropriate. Whatever the case, this was the most forlorn place Neboo had ever set foot in. The uncanny, blood-curdling silence spread through the whole forest. Neboo's body quivered. He was struck with fear. "I wish I wasn't alone," he said, sobbing.

Drying his tears on his velvety bluish-grey jumpsuit, it dawned on him that Alphonse had given him what he needed to make it through this creepy place. He opened his rucksack and grabbed the three bags.

He opened up the one that said #1. It seemed quite the logical thing to do. *The Light*, the tag read. Neboo reached inside and took out what looked like a toy kaleidoscope.

He looked into one end of the tube, the one that had the tiny round circle.

"Amazing!" he whispered. He was now seeing everything in shiny colours. The forest wasn't dark anymore for Neboo McCloudy. All was bright. It was as if the seven colours of a rainbow had sneaked through the foamy branches above.

Okay. So now he could see, and he could avoid the green foam more easily. One problem was solved. But he still didn't know which way to go.

"Should I open the second bag?" he wondered out loud. He figured it was that or, most

157

likely, start walking in circles indefinitely through the forest.

"Let's do this," he said to himself.

He opened bag #2. *The Way.*

It was a small crystal box filled with a sparkling white powder. He put some of the powder in the palm of his hand. The sparkles rose and flew ahead, flowing through gaps in the trees and shrubs. Were they signalling the way forward? With one eye on the kaleidoscope, Neboo followed the sparkles in the hope they would lead him out of the forest.

Yet even with those two gifts, the journey was daunting. The Formidable Forest of Foam was indeed formidable. Meaning it was never-ending, unfriendly and full of unsafe places, like the one right in front of him now. Neboo found himself standing on the bank of a wide stream of oily goop.

"How will I get across this?" Neboo's heart was racing, his legs were wobbling, and his breath was coming in ragged gasps. He was tired and frustrated; he really wanted to give up. For the first time in his life, he wished he could have someone there to hold his hand and tell him that everything was going to be fine. But he knew he had to do this on his own. Somehow, he had to find his courage and cling tightly to it, then maybe, just maybe, he would make it across the oily stream and out of this formidable forest. So, he dared to believe in himself, to believe in hope against all odds. This was the moment when Neboo understood what it truly meant to be brave. His jittery hands went straight to bag #3. *The Changes.*

It was a tiny bottle filled with a blue elixir. He lifted the lid.

"What I am supposed to do with this?" Neboo wondered. "Should I drink it?"

He was about to guzzle it down but stopped mid-air. Neboo remembered what Alphonse had done to create his cape. Alphonse had *sprinkled* the glowing purple liquid onto the old sackcloth.

"I should do the same," Neboo reckoned. He tilted the bottle and a few drops of the blue elixir trickled down and landed on a huge foamy log. Right before his eyes, Neboo saw the foam disappear. Then the log flew over the brook and turned into a pontoon bridge. With wary steps, Neboo McCloudy crossed to the other side.

Soon he discovered all the other handy transformations he could make with this magical potion. The greenish gooey sap became sweet, nourishing honey. Small bushes were changed into clean pillows to rest on, and big leaves became sleighs to skate faster and more safely down the foamy slopes.

A wash of ease swept over Neboo when he made it out of the Formidable Forest of Foam. He put the kaleidoscope, the crystal box and the little bottle away in his rucksack and whispered, "Thank you, Alphonse the alchemist."

As he was starting the propeller's engine, he saw something out of the corner of his eye: a cluster of pearly perfect-shaped clouds. Rays of sheer white light beamed out of them. Was this his destination?

He flew over at top speed. Nimbly, turning off the propeller and jumped onto the clouds. Once he got everything back in his rucksack, he inspected his new surroundings. It only took a quick look around for Neboo to know, right there and then, that he was in Oraland.

At first glance, Neboo saw nothing but white pearly clouds. It was only when he started walking towards the edge of the cluster that he spotted an old wooden chest resting on a small cloud in the distance.

"The Great Treasure!" he shouted. A sizzling ripple of excitement ran through Neboo's entire body.

He rushed to it but as soon as he got there, and to his great disappointment, he saw that the chest was sealed with a thick rope and a tight knot, and beneath that, there was a lock for which he didn't have a key.

He remembered the scroll.

The answer had to be in there.

He unrolled it and read again:

In the skies of Oraland,
Endless fortune is at hand;
The Great Treasure will appear,
If you're smart enough to hear:
You will find the magic key
Inside a clover oozing glee.
If you don't see and you are not,
You will untie the guardian knot.

But there were no flowers there, let alone one oozing glee. His stubbornness made him think harder. He sat on the small cloud, put his elbows on his knees and rested his head on both hands. Then he pondered, analysed, deduced and decoded, and soon after, he thought some more. He stood up and began walking round and round in circles until he wore out a doughnut-shaped groove in the cloud. He read the poem over and over. It was probably the seventieth time he had gone over it when he noticed something:

"If you don't *see*"

No C

"And you *are* not"

No R

He saw it on the piece of paper:

Inside the word *CLOVER* he found the word *LOVE*.

He couldn't disguise the triumph as he said aloud:

"LOVE!"

The rope untied itself, the lock popped, and the chest opened. Neboo could barely contain his excitement. He leant closer and looked inside.

"I don't understand," he whimpered, "what in the world is this thing?"

The wooden chest held nothing but what you and I know to be a hand mirror.

Neboo picked it up and looked into the strange object. This was the first time he had ever seen his reflection, so he didn't realise it was himself looking back. He dropped the mirror and hid inside the cloud. It took a while to find the courage to get out of the cloud. Once out again, curiosity made him pick up the mirror and peep around its border.

"Is this me I'm seeing?"

He looked away and scratched his forehead.

"This can't be right; this can't be me. There has to be a mistake."

Neboo McCloudy looked at himself in the hand mirror once again, then buried his head in his hands as it confirmed what he'd seen the first time. The mirror was doing nothing but showing him who he was. Drowned in sadness, Neboo began to cry.

"Oh no! No, no, no, no, no! What is wrong with my face?"

His was the face of someone who had never smiled before.

He had to do something about it. Still staring at himself in the mirror, he dried his tears and made an effort to find this foreign facial expression he had so long despised. It was one of the most difficult things Neboo had ever done in his entire life. He tussled with his grumpiness, his bad mood and his anger.

"THIS IS TOO HARD!" Neboo cried, flinging the mirror down into the pearly clouds. But he kept trying. He never thought struggling to find a smile would be so difficult. It was like lifting a loaded truck, or attempting to squeeze a watermelon through a keyhole.

He growled.

He clenched his teeth.

His forehead wrinkled.

He was sweating like a hippo.

But then... He remembered... He remembered the huge amount of kindness he had been shown on his journey: the guidance from the selfless carrier pigeon on the Caramel Way, the generosity of Bernard and Babette in Efflo, and the wisdom shared by the unflappable alchemist in Ocelotte. All of a sudden...

PLOP!

A teeny smile popped up on Neboo's face.

"Wow!" Neboo looked at himself in the hand mirror.

Was that a smile on his face?

It didn't feel bad.

It didn't feel bad at all. It actually felt cosy, songful and vibrant. It had a pinch of sweetness and glow in it too. It felt safe.

He decided to attempt a bigger smile.

This time it was a bit easier, tough but not impossible, like lifting a heavy box or touching your nose with your tongue. He thought about what Alphonse had said when they met: "Everything in life can be transformed for the better."

PLOP!

A BIG smile appeared on Neboo's face.

Joy tinkled from toes to head and from head to toes.

What a delight!

He was undoubtedly relishing this. The way

it all felt. The smiles brought a whopping amount of glee to his heart and it made Neboo want to twirl like a ballerina.

He knew he had to go for an even bigger one, a HUGE one.

And he did.

PLOP!

He was smiling with his mouth and eyes and fingertips.

What was this he was feeling?

"Is this…happiness?" he wondered.

Yes.

It was.

Neboo McCloudy was happy.

He liked it.

A LOT.

On his way back to Floccusville, he stopped by Ocelotte to visit Alphonse. Neboo told him about Oraland, The Great Treasure and finding love inside a clover.

"I think I know what the things that truly matter are," Neboo said.

"What would those be?" Alphonse asked, and he drew on his pipe.

"Friends, the good kind. Happiness, the true kind. And smiles, the real kind. But you can swap the words. You know, mix and match. It's still gonna make sense."

"Meaning?"

"The things that truly matter in life can also be friends, the real kind, happiness, the good kind and smiles, the true kind."

"Speaking like a true alchemist... I like that," Alphonse said. "I think those are indeed things that truly matter, Neboo McCloudy."

Lincoln Jax

Life at Wendelin Children's Home has never been perfect, but it is the only one I know. At the moment there are thirteen girls and eleven boys living here, but the number changes. Wendelin is an old, draughty three-storey house. And when I say old, I mean *really* old.

Just to give you a clearer picture, the roof sags and most of the cedar shingles stick up like wonky teeth. The creaking floorboards are always covered in dust and since we usually choose to walk around barefoot, our feet are always dirty. Our bedsheets have stains and the bedcovers smell like old socks and rotten eggs. Yes, even after washing them. They don't wash them often, and even if they do, they don't do it well.

Every corner of every room is a home for a spider. When it rains, which happens often, there are (I counted them) twenty-seven leaks drip, drip, dripping into twenty-seven buckets. It is scalding hot in summer and numbingly cold in winter. But the worst part, at least for me, is that there are so few windows.

Having said all this, Wendelin is all I remember. Apparently – or so Ms Morton, the head of the orphanage, once told me – someone had knocked on the door in the middle of the night and when the night clerk opened the door and saw no one, he looked down to find a baby girl wrapped in a frayed blanket staring back at him with big honey-coloured eyes. Yes, that baby girl was me.

I am ten now, and at this moment I am sitting in the lunchroom, although why we call it the *lunchroom* I'm not sure since we eat all three meals here. I whirl a spoon in my bowl. Let me introduce you to the world's most boring breakfast: cooked oatmeal without any honey, or sugar, or butter. Needless to say, it is quite often served with nothing on the side.

"Lincoln? Are you alright?" Becky, my one and only friend at Wendelin, says as I stare at my ridiculously plain bowl of porridge.

"What?" I say without taking my eyes off the bowl.

"Earth calling to Lincoln Jax! Are you there?"

"Sorry, Beck." I look up and smile at her. "Yeah, I'm fine."

"Are you sure, friend? You don't look fine. That's not your usual smile. I know your real smile and this one isn't it."

"I'm just thinking… I've been thinking a lot lately."

Becky sits next to me. Her face looks puzzled and curious and concerned all at the same time.

"Have you ever wondered what life is like outside Wendelin?" I say. A lump wells in my throat. "I mean…don't you think that life shouldn't be so colourless, dingy and–"

"Miserable?"

"Well, yes."

"Of course I do. But what can we do? We orphan kids, we're kinda stuck here. I don't think wicked adventures, dreamlike voyages and madly heroic quests are in our destiny. Those things are not for us lot."

"I guess you're right. But, Beck, I can't help but feel utterly desolate, confounded and inconsolable."

"Okay, first, I have no idea what those last three words mean but judging from your face it must be the opposite of happy and hopeful. So…" Becky elbows me covertly. "I know what will cheer you up."

"I seriously doubt that, Beck."

"Come on, Linc, let me try. Besides, I owe you for the countless times you did this for me. If I had a penny for every time you made me laugh when I was sad, I would be the richest girl in the city."

My eyes meet hers quizzically. I really don't think she can come up with anything that will get me out of this wretched mood I'm in but hey-ho, let's see…

"Do you want to sneak into the kitchen and steal two bananas to make this breakfast worth eating?"

I was wrong. Becky nailed it! I love stealing stuff from the kitchen. I smile.

"Now there's your smile! Welcome back, Lincoln. Are you ready?"

"Always."

"Let's go then!"

The Invitation

Unfortunately, unlike other times, as I stretch my hand to snatch our two yummy bananas, Becky and I are caught by Gertrude, the cook. Hence why I am currently sitting in Ms Morton's office.

"Lincoln, Lincoln, Lincoln." These are the first three words out of Ms Morton's mouth. I've heard them before. She always utters them like a sort of hopeless sigh. "You, my dear girl, are *quite* the puzzle," Ms Morton says. "A bit of a contradiction."

Ms Morton is the sort of woman who takes great delight in finger-wagging speeches. But, I have to say, I've never heard that phrase before. Where is she going with this? I decide not to say anything. Our eyes lock over her perfectly tidy desk.

"You misbehave," she says.

True.

"You ignore our rules. And if you can't ignore them, you either bend, twist or break them."

Also, true.

"You are always getting into trouble, especially with Becky. You're wild, you never even so much as cringe at the thought of doing something naughty. In short, getting into mischief is your hobby of choice."

What can I say? She is right about all of the above.

"But then, on several occasions, I find you in the library buried in the pages of a book."

Also true. I like to learn. I consider myself a keen logophile. Words can teach you so much about the world. And there's no better place to find them than in a book.

"If I'm not mistaken," Ms Morton continues,

"you have read every single book in our library. Some of them twice… I've checked the log." The corners of her lips twist into a slight smirk.

The selection in Wendelin's library is anything but extraordinary, but Ms Morton is once again right.

"Surely there's not a law against that now too?" I ask her. I try to sound defiant. No idea if I succeed.

"My point is that you are clever. And here's the problem: clever and troublesome is not a good combination. If you keep behaving this way, other measures will be taken. Punishments of the sort no child likes to go through. Am I understood?" Her words come out spiky and vinegary.

Ms Morton has threatened me before, numerous times, but never like this, never with this tone of voice and such an angry look in her eyes. This warning is real. I have heard older kids talk in hushed tones about her punishments, but I never actually believed them. I thought they were just that: silly gossip and rumours. My heart thuds; a cold shiver creeps down my spine. I nod.

"Glad we understand each other. Now, off you go."

I try to hold them in, but for some reason, tonight I shed more tears than I have in my short life. I get out of bed and tiptoe to the only window in the room. All twelve girls are asleep; I try not to make too much noise, though it is almost impossible on this creaky wooden floor. The girls' room is on the third floor. All the way up at the very top of the house.

The window is not that big, but I can see the moon and a few stars shivering in the faraway distance. I sit on the inside sill and press my forehead against one of the panes.

Out of the corner of my eye, I spot an unusually big bird flying towards the house. As it gets closer, I notice it is a white crane. I have seen all sorts of birds through this window before but never a crane. I am sure it is one though, with its stick-like legs and its long neck outstretched as it flies. The bird's feathers gleam in the moonlight and the slow flap of its gigantic wings is graceful and confident.

It lands on a cedar shingle right next to my window. Not only is it looking at me quite intensely but, most peculiarly, it is also holding an envelope in its beak. Despite their intensity, its eyes are friendly. I somehow find myself feeling less alone in the world, not wanting to cry anymore. Something about this bird brings warmth to my heart, a kindness and ease I have never felt before.

I open one of the windows. A cool autumn night breeze seeps into the room. The white crane hops onto the windowsill and drops the envelope right next to me. It reads: *Miss Lincoln Jax.*

Okay. There must be a mistake. It is dark. Clearly I have misread the words. I lower my head to get closer to the envelope and wait for my eyes to adjust. Yep, that is my name right there.

"What in the world is this?" I say almost involuntarily.

"It's an invitation for you."

I snatch a glance around me, trying to beat back my confusion. Too many crazy things are happening in too short a time. My brain is working at full speed to figure out what is going on but fails to find any sensible answer.

"Did you just speak to me?" I ask.

"I did."

"But you're a crane. You squawk. You don't speak."

"My name is Pearl. I come from a place where birds not only speak, but where all other kinds of wondrous things happen."

"What kind of wondrous things?"

Pearl hopped closer and whispered, "Things here unseen and unheard. But of these things I cannot speak. And even if I did—"

"It's not what really matters." These words slip out of my mouth. I knew without asking that I'd finished her sentence. It was as if suddenly things did make a bit of sense.

"You are correct," Pearl says. "What really matters is in this envelope. *Very few people*, and I don't exaggerate when I say *very few people*, get this invitation." She taps the envelope with her beak.

"Why me?"

"You'll find the answer to that question in due time. If you decide to accept."

Pearl's voice is the softest and sweetest voice I have ever heard in my whole life.

"How did you know I'd be by this window tonight?"

"You ask too many questions, Lincoln Jax. Some things are more important than others."

"What do you mean?"

"You're curious. I like that. It's a good trait, but you're also impatient. Patience is just as great a virtue as curiosity."

Before I can say anything, Pearl soars away, becoming a dot, before disappearing into the dark sky above. I close the window and grab the envelope in both hands. I stare at my name for a while, and then trace it with my index finger before summoning the courage to rip the envelope open.

Beyond the Towering Mountains of the East, there is a kingdom.

In this kingdom there are no queens or kings.

There are no thrones, courts, crowns or sceptres.

This is a kingdom beyond what anyone dares imagine.

This is a kingdom beyond all that is magical and fantastic.

It is the dwelling of a great secret, and only you are invited to see it.

Three trials must be passed to reach this realm.

Only a daring, fearless being would embark on this journey.

If you know yourself to be one, follow this path:

Half a mile north of Wendelin, there is a playground.

Between the swings and the seesaw, you will find an arched timber door.

Walk through it and you will find yourself one step closer to your destination.

I must do this. Like now! is my first thought. A way out of Wendelin! A second thought pops into my head: *I don't even know where I am going.* And then, a downpour of questions flood in: am I sufficiently daring and fearless? What if this place is worse than my orphanage? Can somewhere be worse than Wendelin? What if... What if it is the complete opposite of this place?

This last question gives me the answer: I have to find out. I must go.

The Doors

At Wendelin we don't have much. Most of the things we own have been donated to the orphanage.

So, deciding what to take isn't a tough or lengthy process. I take off my pyjamas and put on my green dungarees, which I always cuff above my ankles. Underneath goes one of my two long sleeved T-shirts. I snuggle into my moth-eaten mustard-coloured jumper. Woolly socks and boots on, I am set to leave.

Wait. There is one last thing I must do before I go. I tear a piece of paper from the notebook on my bedside table, and with my only pencil I write: *Beck, I'm going in search of my wicked adventures, dreamlike voyages and madly heroic quests. Remember my real smile.*

I creep to her bed, knowing there is only space for me on this quest, and I leave the note next to Becky's pillow. Guilt tugs at my tummy. I can only hope she forgives me for leaving. My eyes well up as I wave a silent goodbye to my best friend.

I sneak out through the window onto the roof. Once outside Wendelin, it dawns on me... I am free. I am finally free! But, I am also on the roof of an old house. Not too worried though. There is a ladder that has been resting on the side of the house for weeks, waiting for a roofer to come and fix all the broken cedar shingles. So far, no one has come to do the work and Ms Morton left the ladder there in the hope that someday she will get around to dealing with the problem.

Using my hands for balance, I crouch and steadily crawl to the edge of the rooftop. I grasp the ladder, vertigo momentarily making the ground rise up sickeningly to meet me, that awful plummeting feeling. I concentrate on the rungs and climb down the ladder until my feet land on the ground. The thought of using that ladder to run away had crossed my mind more than a few times; I just didn't know where to go. Now I do. I dart north towards the playground.

As I run, I ignore the urge to stop and look around the city. So many things are flashing past my eyes. Things I have read in books but never seen before: a pharmacy, a convenience store, traffic lights, newsstands, bus stops and shops of every kind.

Even though the night is somewhat quiet and only a few cars are around, I use all the zebra crossings. I reckon now is not a good time to break any rules.

When I get to the playground, straight away I start looking for the swings and the seesaw. The first thing I see is a slide, then a merry-go-round, two horse-shaped springers, a sandpit, and aha! Finally, my eyes land on the seesaw and the swings. And what do you know, an arched timber door stands right in between them. A lonely door, attached to nothing, in the middle of a playground.

If I must be completely honest, deep down, I am not sure whether I believed I would see what I'm seeing. But there it is. I am now right in front of the arched timber door. I touch it. It is real.

My hand grabs the round brassy knob and turns it. The door opens surprisingly easily. There is a whirlwind in my chest. I cannot see anything on the other side but I take a deep breath and walk through the open door.

*

The first thing I see is a meadow. It is daylight. Tall grasses, their faded green matches my dungarees to perfection. Thistles, cornflowers and poppies dot the landscape purple, blue and red. There is not a single cloud in the sky.

I turn around to close the door. Behind the door the view I see leaves me completely dumbfounded. Mountains with beaming blue ice on top. Are those the Towering Mountains of the East? They can't be. How did I travel so far away?

As I have said a number of times since this story began: even though I've lived all my life in Wendelin, I've read loads. I once found a dusty old book in the library that spoke of epic tales, legends and folk stories. One of them mentioned the Towering Mountains of the East and how no one really knew what lay past them.

As the story goes, if anyone were ever to cross these mountains, the summit would be seen covered with snow that shines bright blue when hit by the sun's rays. Well, that is what I am looking at right now. It is not an icy sort of blue. It is a glowing deep blue, the colour of sapphire gemstones.

To make matters more puzzling, the book detailed that in order to get from the city to the Towering Mountains of the East, you must travel lots and lots *and lots of miles.*

The journey would go something like this: one must board a train to get through the Arcane Bridge all the way to the Arcane Station. From there one must walk through the Farm Fields of Fleeting Feathers, the Pathway of Pedantic Plum Trees, the Great Grumbling Grassland, the Riveting River Valley, and the Wood of Whispering Weeping Willows. If you've made it this far, you have to climb the Towering Mountains of the East, which as far as I'm aware, very few have done before.

I, Lincoln Jax, just seem to have walked through a door in the city, bypassing all the above and popped up in this meadow.

But even that is not the weirdest part.

I turn around again; the mountains are now behind me, but about twenty steps ahead, there is another arched timber door. This one seems a bit older in design and has a little frosted-glass window a few inches above its centre.

I walk towards it and turn the round brassy knob just like I did with the first one, only to find, this time it is locked.

Okay, let's try this the polite way. I knock three times. No one answers. I wait a few seconds and knock again. Complete silence. I sneak around it. From the other side, it looks the same only without a knob. I circle the door until I am back in front of it.

My palms are sweaty. That is what happens to me when I want something *really* badly *really quickly*. Impatience starts to swirl around in my stomach. I dry my hands on my dungarees and stare at the door. I don't think I am even blinking. The white crane's words suddenly dawn on me: *Patience is just as great a virtue as curiosity.*

Pearl was right. Being all eager and desperate will not get me far. I must think. Properly think. Focus my mind on what I want, which is to open this door. I have to consider all the possibilities before deciding.

An idea pops into my head. I go with it.

I gently knock on the little frosted-glass window. It opens.

The most curious little creature comes flying out and lands on the frosted panes. It looks like a small ermine, but with dragonfly-like wings the size of its body. It is wearing the most peculiar headgear: a purple beret not made of wool but of a softer and glossier material. Two antennae spiral up to where there are two letter Ls, one capitalised, the other in lower case. The curious little creature's white fur has silver flecks that gleam when they catch the light of the sun. Just like with Pearl, this being makes me feel at ease. Unlike Pearl, and despite its size, it also carries a stern and commanding presence. It doesn't scare me. It just prompts me to unthinkingly have a great sense of respect for it.

"Hello. I'm Lincoln."

"I know. You are Lincoln Jax. Welcome. It's nice to finally meet you."

"Finally?"

"I am a *laureline*. We *laurelines* are the sentinels of the three doors. Guardians if you will. I keep watch over the first one. Technically the second, but this is the first trial door."

"Trial door?"

"You can only go through this door if you pass a trial. This is the first portal to Hazel Lands."

"Hazel Lands?"

"Interesting. It seems you only speak in questions. Yes, Hazel Lands. Pearl gave you the invitation, correct?"

"Correct."

I now realise that up until this moment I didn't even know the name of the place I was heading to.

"These are the rules, Lincoln Jax: you'll have to pass through three doors, or portals as we like to call them. Each portal is guarded by a *laureline*. But in order to do so, you must answer a question. If you answer truthfully and rightfully, you may walk through, and you may also ask one question. Are you with me so far?"

"I am."

"You can always go back through the door behind you. Back to Wendelin. However, if you decide to go forwards, you'll be stepping into another realm and it's not so easy to find the way back."

"I want to go forwards." I say this without a shred of doubt.

"Very well. One more thing. It is worth warning you: never betray a *laureline*. No one should want to test our powers."

I believe him.

"Are you ready, Lincoln Jax?"

"Yes."

I think I can hear my heartbeat. Let me rephrase: I am *certain* I can hear my heartbeat. It is pounding so fast, so deeply and so shockingly loud, I am afraid I won't be able to hear what the *laureline* asks.

"This is your question, Lincoln Jax: why are you here?"

"I beg your pardon?"

"Why are you here?" the *laureline* repeats.

I heard right. That is the question. My palms are sweaty again. This time not because of impatience but a fair share of fear and worry. If I get this wrong, I will be sent straight back to Wendelin. But how am I supposed to know the right answer to that?

I take a deep breath. The *laureline* said I must answer truthfully and rightfully. Since I do not know what the right answer is, I will answer with the truth. My truth, anyway.

"I needed to get out of the place where I lived. I hated Wendelin. I had no hope there. Not a single drop. I've got hope now. And I like how hope feels. I like it so much I don't want to lose it again. Ever. You see, I have never felt I belonged to a place. That invitation has changed everything for me. Pearl's visit gave me what I needed: faith to believe that life *could* be different. I'm not sure where I am going but I somehow feel closer to home, if that makes any sort of sense."

"It does. I hereby approve your way forward. You can walk through the first trial door."

"I can?"

"Indeed, you can. And—"

"What? What is it?" Yes, I'm impatient. For me, waiting just sometimes seems impossible.

The *laureline* smiles. "You may ask me one question now."

"Oh. Oh, right. But I have so many." If questions took up space in my mind, there wouldn't be room for anything else right now.

"I understand your quandary. But I can only answer one."

Let us just take a moment to appreciate the importance of choice. Of all the questions that are jam-packed in my brain, I take my pick.

"Why am I here?"

"Same question as mine. Interesting choice, Lincoln Jax. I like it. This is why you are here: a person needs to have a specific set of traits to receive an invitation to Hazel Lands. It is very rare, and it happens once or twice in countless moons. You, Lincoln Jax, were born under the sign of the hazel tree. Inside you, there are three unique qualities: your knowledge, which is unlike any other, your wisdom, which is naturally profound, heartfelt and far-reaching, and your word-wizardry–"

"My word-wizardry?"

"Yes. Your power with words. The way you use and wield words when you speak, write or think is different from other human beings. And if you go forwards, more about this power you will learn. But that is not all. You gain wisdom and absorb knowledge in an almost unnatural manner. You can heighten your concentration at will. You also have a kind heart and you act with good intent."

"But I've been so mischievous at Wendelin," I say, once again interrupting the *laureline*.

"You were naughty in all the ways a ten-year-old is supposed to be naughty. You, Lincoln Jax, like to fight for what is right, you have the most precise sense of judgement and you act free from expectations."

I don't really know what to say, so I choose not to say anything. My mind is trying to process all that has been said by the *laureline*.

"I understand," the *laureline* says as if he were reading my mind. "It is a lot of information to receive. It will take time for all this to sink in."

The *laureline*'s words bring me comfort. Just like with Pearl, I believe him.

"I trust it will," I say to him.

"Are you ready to walk through?"

"I think I am, yes."

"May you journey on safely."

The *laureline* flutters away through the little window. As it shuts behind him, the big timber arched door opens.

I close my eyes and take a deep breath. I take a step. I step again and walk through the first portal, my eyes still closed.

When I hear the door creaking shut behind me, I stop moving and immediately open my eyes. Wow. Wow-wow-wow-wow. What is this place? The meadows are gone. The green grass has disappeared. The ground is white. It is not ice or snow. It is not cold either. It is like I'm standing on sugary sand. The sky is not blue anymore. It is also white and even though there is no sun, it's the most luminous place I've ever seen. I shield my eyes to see if the *laureline* is still here but he's not. Other than the bright white ground and the bright white sky, there is nothing around me. Six thoughts pop straight into my head, one right after the other.

One: *What is this place?*

Two: *What have I done?*

Three: *I am scared now.*

Four: *I shouldn't have left Wendelin.*

Five: *Of course I should have left Wendelin.*

Six: *Which direction should I go?*

I stop thinking and I say out loud: "How will I find the next portal?"

After I utter these words, I see a small shoot pushing its way through the sugary white ground. It blooms right there before my eyes, defying all the sprouting laws of nature. It's a white dandelion. I shouldn't be surprised, given all that I have seen so far, but I am.

I kneel, to look at it closely. It is bigger and fluffier than any dandelion I have ever seen. And here is the really awesome, weird, goose-bump-inducing part... It whispers to me: "Blow, Lincoln, blow."

And I do what it says. And the feathery cotton-like fluff detaches from the dandelion and dances forward in the air.

I follow the tiny woolly seeds. They move fast. I pick up my pace.

They are quite far away from me when all of a sudden they stop moving and fall to the ground. Right where they land, another dandelion grows.

When I get there, I rest my hands on my thighs to catch my breath. I kneel and blow at the big, round, fuzzy dandelion before me.

The woolly seeds fly left this time. They billow fast and I run in their direction so as not to lose track of them. The white sugary sand beneath me crunches. I like the sound I make with each footstep.

I don't have a watch with me, but I think I spend the next, probably, three hours chasing dandelions left, right, forwards and backwards in the vast whiteness. For long periods of time I go forwards. Then I dash to the right for a while and then there are sharp turns this way and that. Always followed by kneeling and blowing, following and running. Until after one last blow, the cotton-like tiny woolly seeds don't go anywhere. They just rise and fall on the white ground next to their stem.

When I raise my head from the tiny cotton fluff on the white ground, I see another arched timber door. Same as the previous one, with an identical little frosted-glass window a few inches above its centre.

I figure I should do what I did with door number one. I knock on the little window. Just like before, a *laureline* — with its little ermine shape and dragonfly-like wings the size of its body, a glossy purple beret and spiralling antennae — flies out and lands on the frosted panes.

"Welcome to the second portal, Lincoln Jax," the *laureline* says.

My brain is still trying to catch up with everything. This must show pretty clearly on my face because the *laureline* says, "Are you alright there, Lincoln Jax?"

"I'm just…relieved and…confused and…very tired to be honest."

"I understand. Those dandelion seeds are fast, aren't they?"

"They sure are."

"It's okay to feel relief, confusion and tiredness. Everyone who is daring and fearless *must* feel all those things in order to become even more daring and fearless."

"They must?"

"Of course."

"I believe you." I really do.

"Are you ready for your question?"

The *laurelines* certainly speak matter-of-factly. They don't seem to engage in any sort of small talk. I don't really mind. I actually kind of like it.

"Yes, I'm ready." I can also get straight to the point.

"This is your question, Lincoln Jax: what holds kingdoms and realms together?"

For some reason, my mind goes straight to Wendelin, and almost without realising, I find myself answering the *laureline*. "I'm thinking about the place where I lived…the children's home, you know. I remember every single time I felt unwanted, unheard or mistreated. I remember the sadness of not knowing what a hug felt like. I remember how much it hurt… I was so lonely. Save for Becky, I had no one. I lived surrounded by other people. But I was alone. Everyone was alone at Wendelin, even Ms Morton; I could see it in her eyes. The only thing keeping that place together were the old walls and a sagging roof. Nothing else. That's not right! That's not how human beings should live together. Whether it's a children's home or a kingdom. It should be held together by kindness, of the greatest form. With love that doesn't need any reason to love. It is just love! That would be a powerful and awesome kingdom. Where people really listen to one another. Where understanding and goodwill are never something you have to ask for." These are thoughts I have never dared explore before. When I finish uttering them, there's a tingle prickling at my skin. I still don't know if the answer is the right one. I stand up straight, on tenterhooks.

I look fixedly at the *laureline*. He meets my gaze.

"Few have spoken so well, Lincoln Jax."

I sigh with relief. It takes me a little while to collect myself and find my next words. "I spoke what was in my heart. Or mind, I should say."

"Exactly. I hereby approve your way forward. You can walk through the second trial door."

"Thank you." My relief has now definitely topped my confusion and tiredness. These last two feelings melt away when I hear the *laureline*'s words, even though I know what's coming next.

"You may ask your question now."

Once again, a choice of questions among so many that are nagging away at me. What is the deal with those magic dandelions? What awaits me on the other side of this door? Will I be able to complete this journey? And maybe the most important question of all: what is Hazel Lands? But I don't ask that, because all I am thinking about is what the other *laureline* said about why I was there.

"The first *laureline* talked about my *word-wizardry*. What did he mean by that?"

Before answering, the *laureline* says, "Why did you choose this question?"

I know why he is asking. "I really want to know about Hazel Lands, believe me. I really *really* do. But right now, I would rather know more about who I am than where I'm going. That's why I asked what I asked."

The *laureline* nods and answers my question. "Word-wizardry is a power. You have it. It is a unique power, Lincoln. A power to wield words into the most extraordinary deeds you can fathom. Once you learn how to use it, you'll be able to do that which is magical, otherworldly and unthinkable."

"Wield words into the most extraordinary deeds. Magical, otherworldly and unthinkable." I repeat the phrases to see if that helps me to understand what the *laureline* means. I'm still not sure I do. Luckily the *laureline* is not done with his answer.

"Word-wizardry comes in different forms. Everyone in Hazel Lands has a different type of word-wizardry. There are those who can word-smith, which is the power to create words that don't exist, but which are needed. There are those who forge spells to right a wrongdoing, or to make someone change their wicked ways. Your particular brand of word-wizardry, Lincoln, is that you can use words to take sorrow away. You will be able to create word-enchantments to help those who feel overwhelmingly sad. Once in Hazel Lands, you will be able to learn all about your power. How to use it, enhance it and practise it till you become a master."

Okay. What does one do when receiving this kind of information about oneself? I know I cannot ask the *laureline* this. He can only answer one question and he has already done that. Do these things really happen? Have I really got a magical power?

I think about the note I left for Becky: I am indeed living a wicked adventure, a dreamlike voyage, and a madly heroic quest. I smile. I bet Becky would say it's my truly real smile.

"Are you ready to walk through?" the *laureline* says.

"I am."

"May you journey on safely."

The *laureline* flies away through the little window. It shuts behind him and the big timber arched door opens.

Three steps and I am on the other side. What welcomes me is utter darkness. The sky is inky black. No moon. No stars. I have no idea where the sky meets the horizon. The ground feels rocky. It's tricky to walk, and my feet stumble a couple of times. As far as I can tell, it is just as black as the sky.

Darkness. The more there is, the less you see. Above, below and all around. Before the stream of frightful thoughts come pouring in, I say out loud, "How do I find the next portal?"

No answer. Nothing. I stand stock-still, waiting. I try to look around. Nothing is happening. Everything is quiet and completely still.

I repeat the question and wait. I dry my palms on my moth-eaten jumper. Impatience is kicking in. *I know, Pearl... I hear you. I should know better than this by now.*

I sit on the hard, uneven ground. My eyes begin to adjust just a little and I see charcoal-coloured stones around me. My hands stroke a few of them. They are rough, sharp and unfriendly.

One thought: *what do I do now?*

The thought of being lost forever in darkness shakes me to my bones. Nerves are chewing at my fingertips and my heart screws tight. There is a part of me that wants to curl up into a ball and wait for someone to come to my rescue. But I know no one will. There is no one here. I am completely alone... Although, what if I'm not? What if I do ask for help? I have always done everything on my own because I have never had anyone to guide me. What if now I do? What if, even in this overwhelming darkness, there is someone willing to give me a hand.

I straighten my back and ready my voice. "I need help. Please. I need to find the third portal. Would someone be willing to help me? Would someone show me the way?"

In the distance, a glow-in-the-dark dandelion starts sprouting. I rise from the floor and walk towards it as it grows and grows until it is taller than me. This must be the biggest dandelion in the world, and I am pretty tall for my age. Besides glowing in the dark, its round puff is the size of a gigantic balloon. Its feathery fluff shines so brightly that now I can see the rocky ground stretching far away into the distance.

I come closer. My nose nearly touches the glimmering fluffy seeds.

"Hello," I whisper.

"Float, Lincoln Jax, float with me," the dandelion whispers back to me.

I grab its thick stem with both hands and wrap my body around it. I hold tightly to it and as I do, the dandelion breaks free from the stony ground and slowly begins to float upwards, lighting the dark

sky as we get higher. The air becomes thinner and a bit colder. I tighten my legs around the stem and look around me. I am flying. I am floating way up high in the air, and from above, it is a world without frontiers. This is the most awesome feeling ever to enter my heart.

The giant glow-in-the-dark dandelion slows down as we near a little grey cloud.

"This is where I leave you, Lincoln Jax," the dandelion whispers.

I really don't want this flying voyage to end. I wish I could keep floating like this for hours or days. But I know this is not my journey's end. This is not my destination. I must keep going. With a mix of determination and reluctance swirling inside me, I release my grip and slide down the stem. My feet land in the grey mushy cloud and I am not in the least bit surprised when I see there is only one thing on it. A door. Yes, an arched timber door with a little frosted-glass window a few inches above its centre.

I am quite familiar with the drill by now. I knock on the little window. While I wait for it to open, I lie on the cloud. My whole body sinks into it. It feels so snug, like a fluffy bear hug. I stare at the dark starless sky above. My pulse slows and the thrill of all that has happened ebbs away.

A creaking sound forces me back to my feet. The little window opens and a *laureline* flies out and lands on the frosted panes.

"Welcome to the third portal, Lincoln Jax."

"What an incredible ride! It's still hard to shake off the excitement of the glowing flying dandelion!" I don't think I have ever shared my feelings in this way with anyone other than Becky, but I've grown fond of the *laurelines* and it feels nice to open my heart to them.

"Oh yes. The glowing dandelions. Best way to travel if you ask me. But I am sure you won't ask me that when the time comes to ask your question, will you?"

"Probably not." I smile.

"Third and final door, Lincoln Jax. Are you ready for your question?"

"I guess I have to be, right?"

"You'd be surprised how many people are not ready to answer what needs to be answered."

"Oh. Really?"

"Really. Lots of people forget the courage they have inside of them. They allow doubt to get in their way. Fear of failure is a terrible thing."

"I'm not in the habit of having that habit. I do believe I am daring. Or at least I do my best to be. I'm not trying to be boastful, I promise. Just honest." I check the *laureline's* face to make sure he doesn't think I am conceited but he doesn't look appalled or anything. On the contrary, his eyes have kindness and acknowledgement in them. "I am ready to answer what needs to be answered."

"Good. In that case, this is your question, Lincoln Jax: what are you going to do with the one life you have?"

It is funny. This is my last question and I

immediately know my answer. No idea if it is right or wrong. But when I heard the question, I knew exactly what I wanted to say. Maybe I have been longing to say these words for a really long time.

"I've never known where I came from. I don't really know where I am going. But I do know this: I want to love. I want to live a good life. But most of all, with all my being, I want to learn who I am and then to only ever be myself. I want to be myself however hard it may be."

"So you're saying you want to be you, always you and nothing but you?"

"Yes. It's very difficult to be oneself, you know. Everyone is always telling you what you should or shouldn't do. What you should or shouldn't say. Who you should or shouldn't be. People like telling other people what to think, or wear, or like. Ms Morton did that all the time. But what if you don't like what everyone else likes? So, yes, I think this is the bravest thing I can do with my life: be myself."

"Lincoln Jax, I hereby approve your way forward. You can walk through the third trial door."

"I've made it?"

"You most certainly have."

"I thought I was going to have to fight wild ogres, slay fire-spitting dragons and defeat trolls of the scariest kind."

"Those are not the true enemies you have to face in life, Lincoln Jax. The three trials are all about confronting and defying your deepest fears. Discovering who you truly are and what really matters. That is the toughest journey one can embark upon. It's what you've done and why you're here."

I made it. My wicked adventure, my dreamlike voyage, my madly heroic quest.

"You may ask your question," the *laureline* says.

"Well, I know I'm about to cross the door and enter Hazel Lands, but I would still like to ask you this, because I would like to walk in knowing where it is I'm walking into."

"That makes sense to me."

"What are Hazel Lands?"

"It is the Knowledge Kingdom. It is the realm of everlasting wisdom, ever-growing understanding and unfading inspiration. It is the land of ingenuity, artistry, imagination and creativity. In Hazel Lands, you will find the most mind-bending wondrous beauty. It has wells of magical ink and clearings of magical dandelions, two of the most powerful sources of inspiration."

"And in Hazel Lands live—"

"I was getting to that."

"Sorry, sorry. I get a bit impatient sometimes. I'm working on that."

The *laureline* smiles. "No need to apologise, Lincoln Jax. In this kingdom live the Hazelanders. They are the most unexpected yet greatest friends you could ever hope to meet. Like, for example, Lola, an astronomer who studies the stars, planets and galaxies in space but is also a genius banjo player. There's Victor, a philosopher who spends most of his time pondering about the meaning of life but is also a prize-winning cha-cha dancer. Or Mr Quill, who arrived not so long ago and is now the savviest book expert in Hazel Lands. There are also us *laurelines*. There's Pearl, the crane, whom you've met, and Abelard, a little white owl who is Alodie's faithful companion."

"Alodie?"

"Alodie, the Knowledge Genie, also known as the Word-Keeper, the Guardian of Language and Words."

"That's the most awesome thing I've ever heard."

"Everything is rather awesome in Hazel Lands. The sky is always orangey-pink, the grass is orangey-yellow and the air smells of recently baked treats. There are hazel trees all over the kingdom and every Hazelander lives in one of them. You will too."

"Like a hazel tree house."

"Precisely. Inside each hazel tree house, Hazelanders can read, think, create, discover, explore and try to find the answers to everything that matters in the universe. Then we share that knowledge with the rest of the realm. This is why this kingdom has always been ruled fairly."

"You practise the noble art of learning."

"Indeed. We value the inquiring mind. Hazelanders are curious people, like you, and are guided by the most ravenous intellectual appetite. And with knowledge and understanding comes love and companionship. No one is ever alone. That is all I can say. But you mustn't worry. Once you are there, you will meet Alodie and she will tell you all you need to know."

"I'm happy to have said yes to the invitation Pearl gave me that night at Wendelin."

"She'll be there to welcome you, along with Alodie."

"I'm worried about one thing though." My mouth purses.

"What would that be?" The *laureline*'s voice is silvery. He sounds as if he has already guessed.

"Once I am in Hazel Lands, could I write a letter to Becky? Just to let her know I'm okay? I won't say anything about the trip, or the doors, or anything. I only want her to know I'm truly happy." I look hopefully at the *laureline*.

"Of course you can, Lincoln Jax. You can write your letter and Pearl will drop it at Wendelin. The white crane knows how to remain undetected when necessary. Do not fret, the letter will be delivered to your friend."

My heart flutters and I realise I am smiling my real true smile.

"Are you ready to walk through?" the *laureline* says.

"I am."

"You have journeyed bravely. Welcome home, Lincoln Jax."

The arched timber door opens and I follow the *laureline* into Hazel Lands.

Another exciting
adventure awaits!

Turn the page for a sneak peak of

The Word-Keeper

Who is Florence Ibbot?

One more day. You just have to wait one more day.

Florence kept repeating this to herself that winter morning. Her trip to Inkwell was only twenty-four hours away. But until then, there was school, and all the good and bad things that came along with it. Florence had figured that there were roughly the same amount of pros and cons concerning school. There were things she found mind-catching, like a good algebra quiz, and things she found rather boring, like setting the gym in order after P.E. There were things that were easy, reciting sonnets among them, and things that were, in her own words, gruelling. Dealing with Gideon Green and the Quarrelsome Queens were two perfect examples of that.

But that morning Florence was too excited to mind either the easy or the gruelling things school had to offer. She was just too happy, exactly as she always was before each year's trip to her favourite place. Had she known everything would change during her stay in Inkwell that December, maybe happiness wouldn't have been her feeling of choice. But she didn't know that, so she sat down for her science class, crossed one foot in front of the other and while she sharpened her pencils she thought about her upcoming trip.

She knew she had to calm down and give her attention to school. Not an easy task, but a doable one for sure, especially considering the fact that Florence had acquired a taste for science. This happened because she liked questions, and science answered questions with evidence. The nature of science, she'd come to notice, agreed with her: the need to understand the world and for it to be logical and fair.

Miss Tolworth walked into the classroom with a pile of books in her hands. Her clacking heels announced her entrance before she could utter the usual "Good morning, classroom." Florence's daydreaming about Inkwell popped like a bubble and she snapped back into school-concentration mode.

"Who here can tell me what an ecosystem is?" Miss Tolworth asked, her shrilly voice working as an alarm clock to wake up the students who were still half asleep.

There was silence in the classroom until Florence said, "It's a biological community of organisms that interact between them and with their physical environment."

"EGGHEAD!" Gideon shouted.

Gideon Green's dearest habit was to torture Florence with nasty barbs. He was a cute boy, but his cuteness was hidden underneath his meanness, so truth be told, he looked like a despicable little rascal. He had stubborn curly hair, plump lips and six hundred and seventy-two freckles on his face.

Most bullies tend to operate where adults aren't present, places like unsupervised hallways, remote corners of the playground or the back of the school bus. But Gideon Green didn't mind if teachers, parents or cafeteria chaperones were right there in front of him. He blurted out the yuckiest, prickliest things without caring who was around. In Florence's case, he usually went for GEEK! or LOSER! And on occasions it was a simple and good old-fashioned NERD!

"Silence, Gideon!" Miss Tolworth yelled over the laughter of the entire class. Florence's golden amber eyes turned deep green.

"Her eyes are changing colour again!" a spindly boy whispered.

"That's because she's a weirdo!" Gideon shouted.

The colour of Florence's eyes did in fact follow her spirit. They were gun-metal grey when she was angry, shifted to the brightest golden amber when she felt pleased or happy, coppery flecks appeared when she was thinking too hard and turned deep green when there was sadness in her heart. And when she felt sorrow, it was a sorrow of the most overwhelming kind. Gideon had succeeded in taking away her happiness.

The worst thing was she could never hit back with the same meanness as him. It wasn't like her and she knew no good would come of it. But that didn't mean she was fine with the situation. Oh no. It was the injustice that got to her. No one deserved to be treated like that. Why did he always get away with it? If only there was a trick to become bully-proofed. Florence closed her eyes and said to herself: *One more day. You just have to wait one more day. Then you'll be in Inkwell and far away from Gideon Green.*

The laughter had died down and everyone was reading up on ecosystems, nutrient cycling and animal species. Because Florence had already memorized that chapter, her mind began to wander as it sometimes did. Complex as an origami butterfly, Florence sometimes got swamped with questions that cropped up in her head. Questions she thought science still hadn't answered: Are penguins confused about being flightless birds that have to swim? Why do people like horror stories? What are the secrets that have never been revealed? How many treasures have never been found?

That winter morning, having brushed off what sadness was left from Gideon's comment, Florence went running to her teacher at the end of the class with, "Why do wolves sing forlorn ballads to the full moon?"

"Florence, for Heaven's sake, where do you find these questions?"

"I don't find them, they find me."

"Well, then hide from them!" Miss Tolworth said. "Don't let those questions find you."

"Why would I do that?" Florence asked.

"Because you are a child. You can't be brooding about those things. You're only eleven years old. There's no need to worry about serious matters," Miss Tolworth answered.

"But..."

"No buts."

"Still…"

"No buts, no stills, no howevers or yets! Do as I say. Go play with the rest of the class and pay no attention to those things," Miss Tolworth said.

But *those things* meant a great deal to Florence. She wanted to know. So instead of going off to play, she went to the school's library and found a book about wolves. Coppery flecks appeared in her eyes as she looked for the answer.

She discovered that what she thought were forlorn ballads was called howling. That's what wolves did to talk to one another. They did it when the sun went down because they were creatures of the night. She didn't find any evidence connecting the howling to the full moon. Turns out, it was just a way of boosting their sound. Wolves pointed their faces to the night sky and that allowed the howl to carry farther.

Now Florence could use the proper word when talking about wolves. They didn't bark or yelp. She figured it was not at all wrong to maybe use the word *bay*, but *howl* was the ideal one.

Florence liked to choose carefully every word she used. She strove to find the word with the right size for the occasion. "Not too small, not too big. It has to be the word with the perfect fit," she often thought to herself.

Her favourite one was *pamplemousse*, French for grapefruit. She loved how that exact combination of letters sounded in her English thinking head. It felt like squishing together dozens of bubbles that wouldn't burst.

She'd never forgotten the first word she looked up in the dictionary: *circus*, a travelling company of acrobats, daring animals and loony clowns that gives merry performances in a large tent. Florence thought it was amazing how so many fun things could fit inside one word. And as a matter of fact, the first word she ever uttered was not *mum* or *mamma*. It wasn't *dad* either. The first word out of Florence's mouth was *hyperbole*, and a cheeky look on her face suggested she'd said it with full knowledge of its meaning: *exaggerated statements not to be taken literally.*

The second and third words out of her mouth came on a day she was very hungry. *Persimmons* and *artichokes*, she said, grabbing one of each from the supermarket aisle. She was colouring a book the day she pronounced her next cluster of words: *flamingo pink*, *myrtle green* and *periwinkle blue*. And the day her parents took her to visit the botanic garden, Florence uttered *yellow primrose* and *autumn catchfly* as she took a whiff of the flowers.

Soon Florence was building sentences like an architect, word upon word, thought upon thought. Now that she was eleven, Florence possessed an unusual verbal extravagance, putting to good use words like *debacle* or *conundrum* or *bodacious*. But this also made her a lonely girl, for not many of the other kids understood what she was saying. She often felt she didn't belong anywhere, like a leafy tree in a cemented playground.

*

Florence closed the book about wolves when she heard the bell ring. She put it back on its shelf and left the library. She crossed the playground where most of the students were still playing as if they hadn't heard the bell and the teachers were trying to herd them back to class. She walked down the hallways till she got to her classroom. Soon everyone else arrived and their ancient history teacher closed the door. Florence sat down and opened her ancient history handbook.

"So my parents gave me all my birthday presents this morning," Tabitha said to Tallulah and Luella as they walked past Florence and made their way to their seats. "I got a piano and a pony, a jewellery box for all my necklaces, because the one I had was already too small, and then a polka-dot skirt and three new lip glosses!"

"Seriously, those are the best presents ever!" Luella said as she sat behind Florence.

"And did I tell you about my birthday party?" Tabitha asked.

Tallulah answered, "We want every detail!"

Florence did her best to tune out their babble. She was known for having a serenity that could calm the most fidgety ferret but it was very hard to be serene around the Quarrelsome Queens. For some unknown law of the universe, Tabitha, Tallulah and Luella were the rulers of the classroom and Florence could not, for the life of her, figure out why. They were conceited, shallow, and loved gossiping. They spoke with irking squeaky voices, bossing everyone around. Their choice of outfits was boringly alike: flared skirt dresses that were always too short or collared shirts with cuffed shorts and knee-high striped socks. They, of course, got a kick out of criticizing anyone who didn't dress exactly like them. And because the Quarrelsome Queens had the habit of biting their nails and all the girls at school were under their ruling, everyone had ragged, uneven fingernails.

When ancient history was over, and so was the non-stop chatter of the Quarrelsome Queens, Florence met with her chess teacher, Mr Rook, and the rest of the chess team to practise for the upcoming championship next semester. Mr Rook was an unbelievably tall man with bulky broad shoulders and a square-shaped head. He spoke with the gravest tone of voice Florence had ever heard and he rarely smiled, but the good thing was he taught the game without overcomplicating what was already quite complicated to begin with. It happened to be the way Florence liked to be taught, with sentences that went straight to the point:

> There are two opponents on opposite sides of a board.
>
> The board has sixty-four squares.
>
> The squares are coloured either light or dark.
>
> Each player has sixteen pieces.
>
> The bishops are the pieces with pointed hats.

Knights don't actually look like knights.

Knights look like horses and can jump like them too.

The king is the most important piece, but the queen is the most powerful one.

The goal of the game is to checkmate the opponent's king.

Checkmate happens when the king is in a position to be captured and cannot escape anywhere.

In order to do this, one has to master the art of planning.

After a seriously tough and ridiculously long game with Abner, the sharpest chess player in the team, where she had to rack her brains only to lose her king in the end, Florence was sitting on a playground bench. She was reading a book that had nothing to do with chess or ancient history or science. It was just a book she was reading for the fun of it. The best kind of book in her opinion.

"Hey, Florence!" Tabitha shouted.

When she heard Tabitha's raspy voice, Florence raised her head, tucked her hair behind her ear and closed the book. She watched as the Quarrelsome Queens approached her.

"Hey, Florence!" Tabitha shouted again.

"I've heard you. What do you want?" Florence asked politely.

"Today is your turn, I want you to do my homework."

So far they had always gone to other fellow nerds with this request, but never to her. Florence closed her eyes and murmured, *"One more day. Inkwell's only a day away."*

"What was that?" Tabitha grunted.

"Nothing," Florence answered.

"Well, you need to do my homework today," Tabitha said.

"No," Florence replied. Her voice was calm. Gideon had already ruined her first half of the morning. She wasn't going to let Tabitha ruin the other half. Florence opened her book and returned to her reading.

"Didn't you hear what Tabitha just told you?" Luella asked as she bit her chipped fingernails.

"I did," Florence answered without taking her eyes off the book. "Didn't you hear my answer was no?"

Tabitha scrunched up her forehead. "Are you saying NO to ME?"

"Yes, I am," Florence answered.

Tabitha's face turned green and it looked like fumes were spouting from her ears. "I'm going to squash you!"

"Yeah! We're going to squash you!" Tallulah and Luella echoed.

"Why would you do that?" Florence asked.

"Because you're saying NO to me and NOBODY says NO to me!" Tabitha said.

"I don't believe that's a valid reason to squash somebody," Florence said.

"But NOBODY says NO to me," Tabitha said.

"That's not true. I just did," Florence said.

"You're looking for trouble, weirdo!" Tabitha said.

"You're looking for someone to think *for* you instead of actually choosing to think for yourself. I won't help you with that," Florence said. She stood up, turned around and walked away from them. She would never give in to their demands, no matter the consequences, for she had decided early on in her life to be *Florence Ibbot* come what may.

Thank you

Helen Hart, Enya Holland and everyone at the SilverWood Books team – working with you is always a pleasure and a privilege.

Lesley Hart – as cliché as it may sound, this book would not be what it is without you.

Kate Haigh – the thoroughness of your proofreading is unrivalled.

Eleanor Hardiman – your illustrations have captured the very essence of each story to perfection and your cover design is stunning.

Sol Jouliá – for being my good and most inspiring friend.

Bonny Paludi – for being my ultimate heroine.

Ale Cavallo – for all the wild and wonderful journeys we've shared together.

And Tomiko – for being the light of my heart.

CPSIA information can be obtained
at www.ICGtesting.com
Printed in the USA
BVHW031409110521
607037BV00005B/141